I0517421

LOST HIS BODY IN MEXICO

MEXICO

Volume 3

the

Escape From Mictlan Trilogy

WILL LORIMER

This book is a work of fiction. Names, characters, businesses,
organizations, places, events, and incidents are the product either of
the author's imagination or are used fictitiously. Any resemblance to
actual persons, living or dead, events, or locales is entirely
coincidental.
Copyright © Will Lorimer
The right of Will Lorimer to be identified as author of this work
has been asserted by him in accordance with the Copyright,
Designs and Patents Act 1998.
All rights reserved.

ISBN: 978-1-8381382-2-6

INKISTAN
.COM

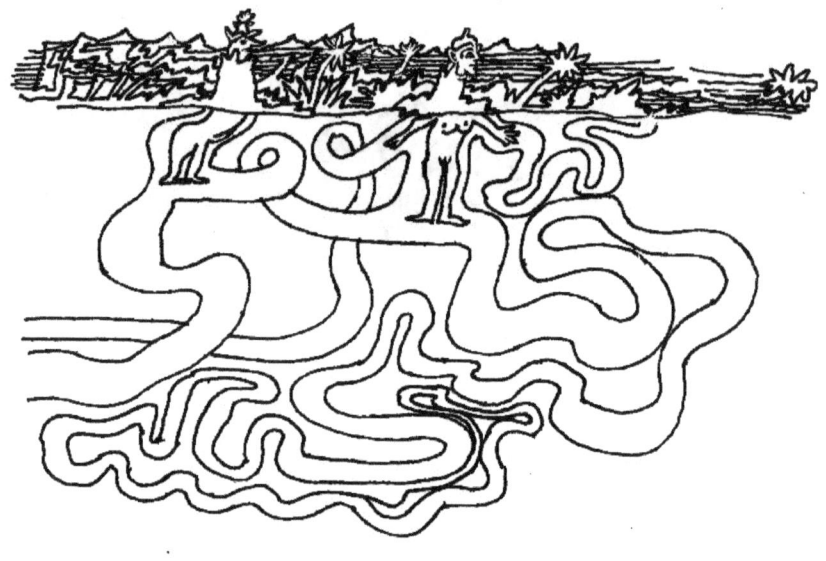

1.

THE STRANGE HOMES OF MR AND MRS CAMOUFLAGE

'*Desayuno! Por los muertos.*'

From the corridor beyond, a call to arms raising a renegade shade from Lord Mictlántecuhtli's penultimate realm, the promise of breakfast, wiping dreamlike recollections – hecatomb realities, gone as though they never were. The one jarring note, the clear plastic envelope on the bed beyond my double's out-flung hand. Inside, a document headed by his double-barrelled name in looping copperplate above an impressive gold seal, embossed with a skull and cross bones. 'Double' looked at it distractedly, putting off checking out the enclosure until later, food being the only thing on his mind just then.

'*Buenas días,* Helga!'

'And to you too, munchkins!' she said, offering up a over powdered cheek to kiss as he stomped into the salon like a matador on the case.

'Mmm! Chanel *Número Venti Cinco!*' Double wrinkled his nose at the cloying taste of face powder on his lips. 'And frying bacon! My favourite smell combination of a morning,' he trumpeted, taking the seat opposite, rubbing his palms with happy enthusiasm. 'I'm so hungry I could eat *una* ...'

'*Toro!*' Helga interjected. 'And what you get up to in the *nacht*,' she said, with an appraising look as she raised a denuded and pencilled eyebrow, 'To be having such an appetite?'

'I dun'no.' Double shrugged, wondering what she had against eyebrow hair, finding her voice more gruff, and Teutonic. 'Dreaming, I guess,' he muttered, pondering her cosmetic changes which, though minor still seemed significant, somehow. 'Who knows? Perhaps I've taken up walking in my sleep.'

'*Ja!*' Helga said, studying his face, thoughtfully. 'The house can affect peoples in that way. It would not be the first time ...'

She stopped as the kitchen door swung back on one of the Malinchés entering, bearing a weighty tray.

Food! Double couldn't take his eyes off this vision of a Hispanic *Nueva* York, rebuilt after the fall – tottering f *tortilla* towers slotting a red sun spilling a sauce boat, set down before a silver platter and a squidgy morass of *frijoles*, crackling with bacon, heaped, sunny-side up, with *huevos rancheros*, just how he liked them, not forgetting *zúmo de naraña* – freshly squeezed – and, glory of glories, strong black coffee steaming in an earthenware jug. A serious business, Mexican breakfast. He was so engrossed he completely failed to notice that Helga ate nothing and only toyed with her helping.

'So, just the two of us,' Double said leaning back in his chair, stretching his arms, and cracking knuckles, clasping fingers behind his neck, 'Tell me, did our friend get away all right?'

'And who is this you talk 'bout?' Helga demanded with asperity that was unusual, even for her.

'You know, Herr what's-it?' Double said, discombobulated by a sudden loss of recall. 'The Austrian chappie questing for ... turtles?' He frowned. 'No, that's not right.'

'You must have dreamed him,' Helga harrumphed. 'The only guest is you!'

That was his second jarring note of the morning. And he had such a clear recollection. A florid face framed by flaring sideburns. Silly bastard, really.

'Yea! A dream! That's it,' Double blustered. 'You're absolutely right about the hotel, Helga, weird vibes. Must be the *emanations*,' he grinned, as a sudden vibration transmitting the floor shook his elbows, leaning on the table top. The cutlery rattled, as if to emphasise his point. 'You know damned fine what I'm talking about,' he continued, rationalising the sudden tremor as a collapse of long-abandoned mine workings far below.

'And what is that?' Helga smiled, all wiles behind her powdered mask, face powder applied thick as icing on a sponge cake.

'Treasure, what else?' he snapped. 'You can't have forgotten our deal.'

'You surprise me!' Conflating, she cast a shadow over the table, as when a thunder cloud, looms out of nowhere on a clear summer's day, 'Perhaps now your holiday it comes to an end?' she glowered.

'What the hell d'you mean, Helga?' Double frowned, at this new line of attack.

She sighed. 'Does your mummy never teach you? Sometimes you have to make effort to pluck the apples from the tree.'

Mummy? Double balked, as into his mind came an image of Helga swaddled in the sump of a narrow wooden boat, lying with her bandaged head propped against the prow, gold coins in her eye sockets, winking back at him where he stood in the stern, leaning on a pole, punting slowly across inky water into a fog bank delineating the limits of memory. What was that about? he shuddered, feeling as if Ixotl, the spotted dog of Mictlán had just peed on his grave. This morning he was even weird to himself, and the day was hardly yet begun. Emanations from below? Double doubted it. That bitch across the table, then? The split between the sexes, widening to an unbridgeable gulf? That time of the month come round again, the full moon bringing on the doomy feeling induced by proximity to blood tides. Periods, he reflected, give women the acuity to see beyond temporal limits, like the curtains of conditioning part a crack. Or crack *ajar*? Perhaps she knew something he was blocking out? Locked away in his parturiated brain, just like every other man, more uncharted regions than the dark side of Neptune, that was for sure.

'And what's apples got to do with it, Helga?' he countered, combatively.

'Maybe more than you know!' she snarled, taking the bait. 'The golden apples of the sun? You never hear tell?'

'Nope,' Double grinned, leaning back in his chair, defying her with folded arms.

'According to the ancient European legends, beyond the setting sun lies paradise and the orchards I speak of, guarded by the three daughters of *nacht*.' She thumbed towards a shuttered window. 'The same mountains closing in the town.'

'You mean *las tres hermanitas*?' he said, wondering why the window shutters were still closed this late in the morning.

'What other mountains do you think I am talking of?'

'So!' he smiled, changing tack, 'What's this, ah ... west-end Eden,' he said, feeling an odd unease creeping on, 'Got to do with the, um ... ah, treasure?'

'Maybe everything, maybe nothing,' she giggled gaily, switching masks and moods. 'In the stories there are fourteen, you know.' She frowned, her face powder cracking some more as her forehead furrowed.

'Fourteen?' He reiterated, recalling Cantina Joe's pronouncement on the subject. 'I thought there were thirteen?'

'Yes,' she nodded, 'Thirteen blinds, each without substance.' Her lips curled, advancing the tracery of cracks across her powdered cheeks. 'Just like the empty promises of the church.'

'And the fourteenth?'

'Ah,' she smiled, '*La catorces*, the only one worth having, the legacy of *ventura*.'

'You mean "lucky"?' he said, noticing that now her face powder was falling in flurries of tiny flakes onto the table cloth.

'That is what I say,' Helga scowled.

'And who was he, this "lucky fourteen"?' Double said, wondering if this all connected with the shot-out sign by the rail track in the desert and its bullet-riddled legend, '*Catorces*'.

'A black slave who won his freedom when he pointed out to his master the silver that would make all their fortunes, cooling in the ashes of the camp fire,' she said, suddenly, unaccountably nervous, reaching up with her big hands and smoothing her tied-back ... *black* hair, which Double suddenly remembered had been blonde before. 'But you distract me.'

'Eden, wasn't it?' he said, trying to regain focus. Women, you never know them really, he reflected, Most of all not this *bruja*, black to her roots and beyond. Dyed of course, he rationalised, otherwise her hair could not have changed colour overnight –

Little did he suspect there was another, altogether more strange explanation.

'Ah yes,' she beamed, precipitating a further fall of face powder. 'The garden, of course, is long gone. The Spanish, they see to that!' she sneered, her mood down-shifting, alarmingly. 'Those conquistadors and their descendants, slash and burn, turn the Virgin to desert. But the temple to her daughters remain,' she beamed, upshifting, again.

'Where?' he groaned, certain the foregoing was a canard.

'Here, you fool,' she said, knuckling the table top, silvery white flakes dancing to her command.

'No,' Double shook his head, 'Credulous and a fool I may be, but you can't expect me to believe that.'

'Why not? Is the custom in Mexico,' she sniffed. 'Cathedrals on pyramid-es and always those on older structures, like the layers of a pavlova pudding. Why not this house, *la Castilla de la Dinero*, on the temple the

Egyptian colonists dedicate to the golden apples of the sun?'

'I've had enough,' he said, looking away – anywhere but at the cracking medusa mask of her grossly powdered face. Stone, I'll turn to stone, he thought, unless I get the hell out now.

'Do as you like,' she said, catching on fast. 'But first,' she gestured towards the mess of plates on the table, 'You must clear these things away and wash up in the kitchen. Malinché has gone off for the day. It is time you earn your keep, do not you think?'

Returning, after a few minutes, Double sensed she was in a better mood, as he pushed in through the salon door.

'You finish already?' she smiled down at him.

'Yup,' he nodded.

'The plates are clean?'

'Spotless,' he said, entirely insincerely.

'And the ones from before?'

'With the others in the rack.'

'You do not put away?'

'I didn't think that's what you wanted.'

'Next time you polish and put away. Promise now.'

'Yes, absolutely,' he muttered, finding her overbearing as ever. 'Can I leave now?'

'You go to get drunk?'

'That depends,' he shrugged, angling shoulders towards the salon door.

Helga sighed. 'I suppose if you must, you must. Come,' she said, standing up, 'I go with you, I have to make sure the sign is still up outside.'

'A sign for what?' Double said, as she pushed past and led the way up the long corridor.

'To keep the perverts away,' she cast back over her sideboard of a shoulder.

'What perverts?' he called after her, trotting to keep up.

'Perverts?' she snorted. 'Pilgrims? What is the difference? You do not notice them swarming like flies in the street?'

'How could I when you keep the shutters in the salon closed,' he panted, as her pace increased.

'I do that so they cannot stare in the windows. So nosey the holy fools are, always judging,' she sniffed, slowing, as she neared the end of long corridor.

'What's the occasion?' he asked, following her into the lobby, which became quite crowded when taking into account the old retainer in his dusty suit of conquistador armour on sentry duty behind the bolted door.

'Tomorrow begins the festival of Shem up at the cathedral,' Helga said reaching towards the door, 'Twenty thousand pilgrims in town tonight. Three days it lasts,' she whirled around, 'But this year I do not think it goes well.'

'Why not?'

'Because this time the Black Friars refuse to let the pilgrims kiss Shem's sacred shin bone.'

'Shin bone?' he laughed.

'That is what I say.' She scowled down at him. 'The Black Friars use it for divination.'

'I thought the church authorities proscribed that, along with necromancy, black magic, voodoo and the rest.'

'The Friars are Shemites not Catholics.'

'Of course,' Double nodded, puzzled he could have forgotten such a salient fact of the town. He stood back as she drew the long bolt and turned the big key in the old brass lock.

Holding the door ajar, she leaned her head around the jam. 'Good, still there,' she announced over a clamour of discordant chants, distant shrieks and wild hosannas coming from the street beyond.

'The sign?' he ventured, determined to stay on good terms before leaving.

'Ja, it say "cerrado",' she smiled, pulling open the heavy door. 'I keep the hotel closed for the whole festival.'

'Sounds a good idea,' he said, squeezing past her into bright opaque light outside, swirling with dust raised by thousands of shuffling feet.

'Don't get too drunk, munchkins,' she laughed, slamming the door before he had a chance to step down onto the street.

2. JOE BUTTS HIS NOSE IN ...

Shunted from the doorstop into the street by the heavy door impacting his rear end, Double stumbled over a shaven-headed penitent dragging himself along on bloodied hands and knees, lashing his back with a barbed flail, between prostrations.

'Jaime!' he blurted, pushing himself up, coming face to face with the slavering flagellant. But instead of smiling in recognition, as might have been expected, the self-abuser merely scowled, and averted his bruised, blood spattered face.

'Fuck you!' Double cursed to no effect, minded of a worm, watching the pilgrim's humping progress, bumping his forehead against the cobbles in time to the happy hand claps of the sack-clothed choristers blocking the street. Above them, stretched between poles, was a banner, flapping in the wind. Looking up he noted its canvas was crudely decorated with a long, pale skeletal leg, surrounded by a spectral green halo, which he took to represent Shem's sacred shin bone, meaning that the Choiristers, below, repetitively singing, what sounded like, 'Gory Glory *Angelitos*, were fucking Shemites.

For a moment Double felt like giving up the ghost and abasing himself to a god he couldn't comprehend, just like all the pilgrims, but his need for a drink in the *cantina* was too strong to join in the fun. Besides, he was desperate to offload to Joe about his narco-nephew. Jaime, last seen – discounting a dream he only dimly remembered – fleeing a battle back in *Happy Valley*.

What the fuck had happened after that? Double wondered. All he could recall was a deafening barrage of explosions; and standing side by side with Jaime in the downdraft of descending black helicopters, before being pursued by into caverns. Then nothing ... absolutely bloody *nada* ... Until, he woke that morning with the most enormous appetite. As if by some incredible feat of somnambulism, overnight he had re-returned from Happy Valley, over the saw-toothed mountains, back across a fucking Norwegian glacier, for Christ's sake, – and then broken into the hotel. Impossible – but how else to explain wakening in his bed? Perhaps those caverns in the Narcos' canyon, led into the lair of one those mythical birds of Joe's tall tales, and he'd been carried over the *cordilleras* in great claws. A ridiculous notion, but while he was on the subject, what were they called? Of course, the *tzitzimime*! Absurdly, Double felt a double-glow of satisfaction, remembering not only the local name of the giant birds the Austrian chappie had insisted were pterodactyls, but also the mad aristo's title, Von Hapsburg, last seen leading the helicopter attack against the Dutch dopers of Happy Valley.

Pulling himself together, Double sighed, sure all the *sappatistas* were dead now, including poor, poor, Jaime. Time to get that drink in the *cantina* and catch up with Joe, he reminded himself, body swerving an reliquary salesman rattling bones in his face, like every other god-struck mendicant in his way, dusty after the long pilgrimage up from the plains – the majority wearing ecstatic expressions, faced lifted towards the sky, unlike the down-cast flagellants, on bloody hands and knees, their faces filthy, flat and drained. The procession flowing around the bandstand in the Plaza de la Revolución, where Gomez's victims were buried, and past the Cathedral steps in the direction of three purple peaks like three church spires, framed the slot at the end of the street, where it looked like a large marquee was pitched in the waste ground, at the edge of town

Feeling like he'd crossed a bloody Rubicon, instead of merely the width of a narrow cobbled street, elbowing aside the last *Angelito* chorister blocking his way, Double pushed through the half doors and stepped down into the hole-in-the-wall establishment. After the clamour and dust outside, inside was peace and serenity. Not a pilgrim in sight, he observed thankfully, his eyes adjusting to the dim light. Unusually Joe not around. Instead, one of the Malinchés behind the bar, taking his order like he was a total stranger.

'*Una doble, señor*,' she smiled surgically, setting down a glass he wished was as clean as her gleaming teeth. '*¿Nada mas?*'

'*Si*,' Double pouted. '*Un pocito beso, por favour*,' he said, surprised at the look of mounting fury he got from her gold-irised eyes. He had only asked for a kiss.

Feigning indifference, taking his drink, he sauntered over to the table by the warm stove in the corner, pulled out a chair and sat down with his back to the bar, wondering whether he'd fantasised the whole scene in the bed with her two sisters. Just like he'd dreamed up old bugger-lugs Baron Von Paedo, he reflected, conjuring his face in the dirty glass cupped between his hands, pooled in oily *mexcal*, sharing murky depths with a worm; silly bastard, really, with his ridiculous nineteenth-century sideburns, waving back from a precipice, unmindful of the native boy rearing up behind, curtain clouds closing on his view ... then a knee knocking into his elbow, drink and a worm slopping the table as he whirled around angrily.

'Holy shit!' Double gasped, at finding himself face-on to a porky barrel-busting belly button beneath a denim shirt. 'Joe, it's you!'

'*Perdon*,' Cantina Joe salaamed, holding one hand to his forehead and a frothing beer glass out in the other, bowing in the manner of dipsomaniac Muslim mullahs. He called back to Malinché behind the bar, '*Una doble mescal sin gusano, por el señor.*' Grinning broadly he then gestured grandly towards the chair opposite, '*¿Con permisso?*'

'Of course,' Double said, regarding the worm spilled from his overturned glass, side-winding drunkenly across the table, remembering his first time in the bar, and Joe's dire warnings about the worm of the devil, lurking the murky depths of every bottle of local *mescal* – sure felt like he hadn't another friend in the world.

'It's been so long,' Joe beamed, 'But what is the matter, my friend?' He leaned closer, 'Looks like you bounce from the *malo* side of the *cama* this morning.'

'Yea, like a human cannonball, up an atom and out the back door,' Double said sourly, looking away, his eyes drawn by a delectable posterior – Malinché bent over the table, wet cloth in hand, pouncing on a saloon wriggler. 'That hotel has weird vibes, Joe,' he went on, as Malinché returned from the bar and set down another *mescal* on the table before him, 'I have these crazy dreams I can't remember for the life of me.'

'*Es importanté* you try. For the dreamer, loss of recall is like forgetting his name.'

Double laughed, at last, his bad humour evaporating, 'So that explains why I don't recognise myself this morning.'

'I know who you are,' Joe said coolly, crafty eyes intent, over a frothy rim.

'You do?'

'From the first moment, my friend.'

'*Por favor*,' Double pleaded, only half-jokingly. 'Enlighten me, *maestro*.'

Joe thumbed over his shoulder at the hotel. 'That first time, when I see you with Helga, I recognise the template.'

'Don't you mean my "basic type", Joe?'

'*Es* close, but template *es* better,' Joe chuckled. 'Template memories, or memory templates, that *es* the diddle.'

'The word is *riddle*,' Double interjected. 'One that is beyond me I'm afraid,' he sighed, 'Those memories are buried just too deep.'

'¿*En serio?*' Joe lofted bushy eyebrows. 'You think I don't understand your connection to Helga?'

'You do?' Double blurted.

'Sure,' Joe said easily. 'There are many similarities. Not the height of course, but you have the same eyes as she had.'

'Had?' Double repeated, feeling naked and exposed 'What do you mean?' he said, suddenly afraid.

'My friend,' Joe said sadly, 'You must still be in shock. During your mother's funeral, when the sky went dark as the asshole of night, all through the hailstorm with only lightning to see by, I am looking everywhere for you.'

'Now you're kidding me,' Double said. 'I just had breakfast with Helga in the hotel. She was alive as ...'

'My friend,' Joe interjected firmly, 'Your mother is dead as a doornail and buried ten times more deep. For months now the hotel has been closed, with only the Malinchés keeping it dusted. But you know all this.'

'I do?'

'Easy, my friend.' Reaching out Joe laid a broad hand on Double's shoulder. 'I believe you. Tell me, how did Helga seem when you left her in the hotel?'

'Same as ever. Well, maybe not,' Double hesitated, 'When I think about it, she did seem a bit odd.'

'Describe her,' Joe insisted, gripping Double's slumped shoulder.

'One thing, she had black hair. Dyed obviously.'

'Are you sure it is not a wig?'

Double scratched his temple, uncertainly. 'I don't know.'

'Anything else?'

'Well, her face powder I suppose.' He chuckled, 'You know it was pasted on so thick she reminded me of a layer cake. As she spoke, it flaked and fell in silver flurries. I couldn't take my eyes off it. Perhaps she's got leprosy.' Double, grinned, 'What do you think?'

'No, not, leprosy my friend,' Joe smiled sadly. 'Your mother wears make-up and a wig to cover the fact she is a ghost.'

'OK, she's a ghost?' Double said, realising with sudden certainty Joe was absolutely right. 'But why then has she returned to haunt me?'

'Could be something you have done?' Joe raised bushy eyebrows. 'Or not done?'

'Like what?' Double said, as a pair of winking gold coins appeared in his mind's eye. *A clue, he knew.*

'Perhaps *es* because you miss the funeral?'

'No,' Double shook his head, 'I don't think so.'

'Maybe something you forget?'

'Like in a dream?'

'Maybe,' Joe nodded gravely, reaching for the bottle between them.

'I know it's something to do with tokens,' Double continued, aware of the importance of dissembling when it came to the subject of gold. 'I remember she's lying stretched out in a narrow boat, with a token waxed into each eye socket. They twinkled at me out of the darkness as in the prow as I stood in the stern, punting the little boat through fog across a broad black river. What do you suppose that was about?'

'*Es* the Black River of Mictlán, my friend,' Joe said, refilling Double's glass. 'You were together for her last journey.'

'Please don't say that,' Double shivered.

'*Es* true,' Joe insisted gently.

'I know,' Double said, staring into his glass. 'I wanted to return for the tokens, but ...'

'*Es* because the tokens were your fee,' Joe interjected.

'But I never again could find the place where I put her.' Double looked up – anywhere but at his memories of Mictlán, welling from a bottomless pool in a dark cavern deep below Happy Valley, 'Joe, why has she come back?' He bunched fists, 'What the hell is she after?'

'You,' Joe smiled. 'The essence of you.'

'I don't understand.'

'My friend,' Joe sighed, 'You have to take into account how it *es* with vampires.'

'She is a *vampire* now?' Double's voice upped in pitch.

'In a figure of speaking,' Joe raised a hand. 'Allow me to continue. Only by stealing the essence which she lost giving birth can she become flash and blood again.'

'The phrase is "flesh" and blood,' Double snapped, '*Flesh* and blood.'

'Thank you,' Joe nodded, imperturbable as ever.

'So what is this *essence* exactly?' Double asked, his heart skipping a beat as in the distance, the bell of the cathedral, pealed the quarter hour.

'There are many names for it. Middleganger, Fetch, Ka. To the native peoples of Mexico it *es* the Nagual. In a way, you could say it *es* like the soul Christians believe in, but so much more.'

'So,' Double sighed heavily, 'Now, I have to protect my nagual.'

'Yes,' Joe said, staring at Double oddly. 'Yes, you, most of all.'

'Oh god,' Double blubbed, suddenly overcome, covering his face with his hands. 'I still can't believe Helga's dead. She always seemed so ... so bloody permanent.'

'Don't you remember, the last time in my bar, you yourself are telling me she has cancer.'

'And when was that?' Double demanded though his parted fingers; hating Joe at that moment, wanting, as he did anything but plain unvarnished truth.

'Before you take off with the old *gringo*.'

'And what the fuck was I doing *taking off* with an old *gringo*?' Double demanded angrily, as into his mind appeared a grizzled face incised by the magenta light of the sun, setting over a maze of snow-capped canyons in the far distance.

'Looking for Jaime, what else?' Joe leaned closer, 'My friend, I mean to ask, do you ever find him?'

'Oh god. Joe,' Double's face crumpled, 'I meant to tell you, when I came in ... I keep seeing him in the street, in dreams. Everywhere I look. But he's dead, I'm certain of it.'

'You don't sound so sure, my friend.' Joe took Double's hand between his. 'You must explain.'

'There's not much to tell. He was showing me the sights of Happy Valley, then,' Double gulped, 'The Baron and his men descended from helicopters, there was fighting, explosions, and ...' he gulped again, 'and then I found myself back in the hotel. I don't know how.'

'Start at the beginning,' Joe insisted. '*Es* always the best way.'

However, before Double could provide a clear account, first he had to disentangle the details of battle, and his shame of fleeing it, from memories flooding in of his time as a shade in Mictlán, which were somehow bound together with his twin's dream of Jamie's trial. Hearing him out, Joe was patience itself, now and then topping up his troubled friend's drink, never a twitch of incredulity on his boozy hooter, wearing only concern on his weather beaten face, as Double went on endless digressions of conversations with demons and of transporting stiffs to their last resting places on a far shore. But all the while, talking, sorting his memories into sequential order, one thought kept compressing the remaining functioning hemisphere of Doubles divided brain.

Coming to the end of his account, mid-afternoon, mindful of the death certificate in his room back at the hotel, at last Double was able to ask, 'Joe, do you think I am dead?'

'That depends on the way you see yourself, my friend.'

'How so?' Double frowned.

'Here in Tláltipec, the ultimate level of Mictlán, you, me,' he gestured, 'Those pilgrims out there, everyone here,' In a sideways look he included Double, and Malinche, occupied behind the bar, 'are the living dead. All on our way,' he indicated with a finger, pointing to the floorboards between their feet, 'Down to the next level below the mines, unless ...'

'Unless what?'

'That is up to you to find out, my friend. It is *la catorces*, the ultimate prize,' Joe smiled enigmatically. 'But for now I have to make plans to free Jaime from those *pinché* Black Friars.'

'But the trial was my twin's dream, nothing more,' Double protested.

'You are wrong, my friend,' Joe insisted, patting Double's s shoulder comfortingly. 'The messages of the dreaming twin are always true.'

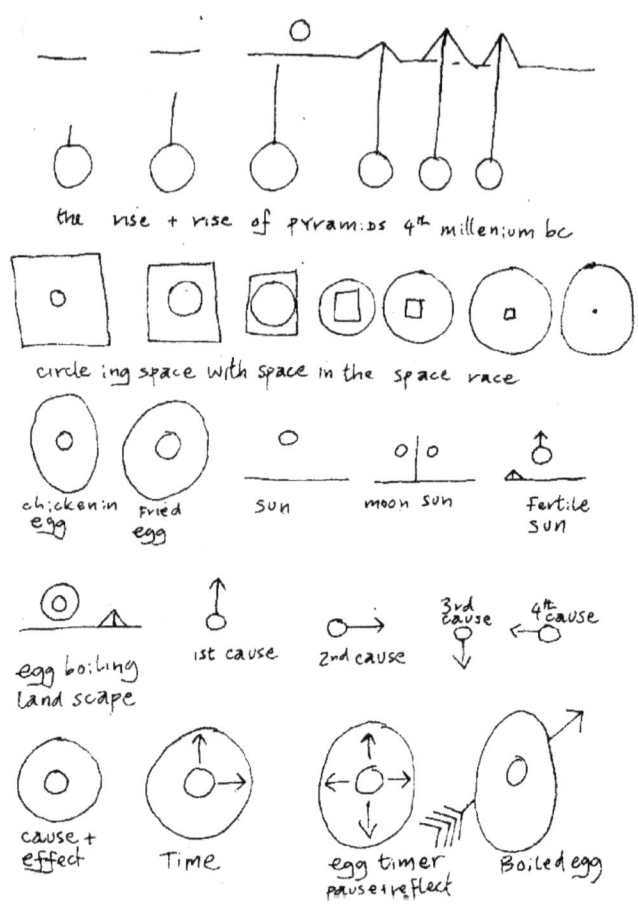

the rise + rise of pyramids 4th millenium bc

circle ing space with space in the space race

chicken in egg   fried egg   sun   moon sun   fertile sun

egg boiling land scape   1st cause   2nd cause   3rd cause   4th cause

cause + effect   Time   egg timer pause + reflect   Boiled egg

From the journals of Menes, a Pharaoh of the Inkethaton Dynasty

3. THE INEXORABLE RISE OF THE INKETHATON DYNASTY

What did he expect? Helga and *las Malinchés* haunting desolate corridors? A hunted feeling descended as he snuck in, sneaking backwards glances, 'till at last to his room, safe and with time to think.

'What the ...? Who the ...?' Double gasped, stepping inside, only then understanding that the tall stranger facing him across the room was in fact himself, reflected in a long mirror, fixed in his absence to the front of the wardrobe, giving it the appearance of an open door. Standing framed in the gap, Double's double, wearing his *'I know something you don't know expression,'* to which Double took instant exception.

What was it about himself, he wondered? Why did he have to look so self-important and uptight, when in reality he was confused and in need of help? Even his own name escaped him, as he found himself fixated – a double in double trouble, unable to break eye contact with his reflection and look away. Until, with a superior smile, his mirror counterpart obliged, looking pointedly towards a clear plastic envelope interleaved in a paperback book laying on the bedside table.

Intrigued, putting aside the envelope for a moment, Double flicked through the yellowing pages of an early Penguin paperback edition of *The Lawless Roads*, a novel by Graham Green, which, he noted, was set in Mexico of the 1930s, during the Cristeros insurgency, when religious fanatics waged war against the state, which had banned public religious worship. All well and good, Double thought, but, in his present situation, not exactly relevant reading material. Perhaps something more pertinent was to be found in the envelope? But then, as he reached towards it, he glanced up, realising with a start there was no reflection in the mirror before him, that it *was* in fact a door, open to another room, identical in every respect but one. Namely that he was standing where he was and not *there*. Madness, taking him at that moment, for, without a second thought, overriding the protests of his rational mind, he stepped through the mirror to the other side, experiencing a flash of light from within or without – he couldn't tell – as he did so.

He was reaching for a similar clear plastic envelope interleaved in a paperback novel of the same title and author, laying on an identical bedside table, when a familiar 'Coo-ee,' not heard since he was a baby boy resounded from a distant quarter and demanded his immediate attention.

'Helga,' he exclaimed, reassured to see her hair was blond again, though upon his second glance, noting, as she looked round from rummaging in an open cardboard box set on the polished dark oak of the old sideboard, that her hair was silver at the roots.

'Ah, there you are, munchkins,' she smiled, only then revealing her canyon cheeks in the craggy escarpments of her time-reconstructed face. 'Why do you not answer the first time I call?' she frowned. 'This box is heavy, you know.'

'What's in it?' he asked, keeping a safe distance, in case her antique condition was contagious.

'Souvenirs,' she cackled, passing over something small wrapped in tissue paper. 'I bring from my room to show you.'

'This is a souvenir?' he said disbelievingly, discarding the paper wrapping distractedly. 'Looks like ten-thousand-year-old biltong,' he muttered, turning over in his open palm, regarding a blackened shrunken object, sheathed at one end in silver, the polished metal hallmarked with miniature symbols that he read to be an eye in a triangle, above what looked like an ink jar and below that a feather, which he suspected symbolised a writing quill.

'You are not far off,' she rasped, looming like the cracked shade of an antique standard lamp, standing looking over his shoulder, 'But not so old.'

'It looks ... mummified,' he frowned in reaction to a word he had come to dislike for an obscure reason that eluded him. 'Shit, I know what this is,' he said, revolted, 'Ancient Egyptian, yes?' He scowled, wrinkling his nose, holding it away.

'No, I mean for you to keep.'

'You mean it's a present?' he said, looking up at her craggy face, pockmarked as a cliff, undermined by time and tide.

'What a clever boy,' she said, clapping, disturbing the configurations of the veins on the fly-blown parchment of the back of her hands.

'A fucking penis!'

'A *sacred* penis,' she insisted, every wrinkle of her collapsed face registering indignation and hurt. 'You should not be so disrespectful, that belonged to the Founding Father.'

'The Founding Father?' Double frowned. 'Of what?'

'The Americas, of course, you silly boy.'

'Oh, come on!' he laughed.

'Be very careful,' she growled warningly, 'That it is a most powerful penis.'

'So who exactly was this *Founding Father* of the ... ah ... Americas?'

'A pharaoh of the Inkethaton Dynasty. He founded a second empire in the "Lands of the West" and retired there. Here, to this town, only then it was a temple. This is true, so don't shake your head. The Father of History wrote this.'

'Herodotus?' Double snorted. 'I don't think so. And anyway, even if he did write that, Herodotus is also known as the *Father of Lies*.'

'I do not believe you!'

'Now *you* don't believe *me*!' Double laughed. 'OK, supposing I were to accept all that you claim, what I still don't understand is why you would want to give me this,' he brandished the relic before the three ringed circlets of the hag's hollowed eyes, 'I mean, why, for god's sake?'

'Because of your injury you are telling me of when your wife she ...'

'Enough of that,' Double shouted. 'I'm trying to forget my past.'

'But it will help. I promise.'

'Well, even if I did need help, what am I supposed to do with it?'

'As you like. Chew it, keep it in your pocket. Whatever way you use it,' she shrugged, threatening the structural integrity of her shoulders, 'A pharaoh's penis has great restorative powers.'

'So why haven't you used it?'

'Because I wasn't born with one, silly boy.'

Dismissed, but not downhearted, Double decided against returning to his room, and instead, chose the path to redemption. The only place he knew, a hole-in-the-wall establishment just across the street. But first he had to return something to its former owner.

'Where do you want me to put it?' Double said half-jokingly holding up the shrivelled relic, addressing his reflection in the dull shine of the breastplate of the retired old soldier, suited in conquistador armour, marking time, standing guard behind the lobby door.

'*You need it more than me.*'

'What?' Double gaped, glancing to either side, checking no one else was there.

'*I said, you need it more than me.*'

'This is the mummy speaking?'

'*Yes, my son,*' the mummy rattled. Despite his pharaonic status, his voice tinny and not at all impressive, Double considered, listening with an ear pressed to a tarnished breastplate.

'You're not my father, by any chance?'

'*No, my son,*' the mummy replied with a dry chuckle. '*Though* he *is my son too.*'

'Blood son?' Double interjected, keen to get this right.

'*There is no measure other than ink.*'

'I don't understand.'

'*I was the scribe who wrote, I am pharaoh that I am. And lo, so it was.*'

Was that a sigh Double heard?

'*Things were easier then.*'

'And I am your son?'

'*The last.*'

'The last?'

'*The end of the Inkethaton line.*'

'So,' Double paused, 'If I'm the last, then you must be ...?'

'*The first, my boy. The very first.*'

'First and last? Then we're like book ends.'

'*More than book ends, son. Mucho mas.*'

Double was back in his usual corner of the *cantina*, sticking to his resolution of staying off the *mescal*, when Joe ambled over.

'Please,' Double said, gesturing to the chair opposite. 'Still no news of Jaime?'

'My friend, no news is good news where he is concerned,' Joe said, stooping to add two more beer bottles to Double's growing collection on the table.

'Really?' Double said, refilling his glass. He had been trying to decide whether it was half empty or half full. 'You are not worried?'

'No more than usual,' Joe said, sitting down. He nodded towards the hotel across the street. 'Everything OK with Helga?' he added, lowering his voice.

'Yes. No,' Double grimaced. 'You know, one minute, nice,' he shrugged, 'The next, ice.'

'Be careful, my friend, that *bruja*, she *es* full of surprises.'

'What should I watch out for?'

'Bait!' Joe smiled grimly. 'With hunters *es* always the way. The trap can be anything ...' He frowned. 'I know Helga and her stories, some I expect I even invent myself.'

'How so?'

'Once I call her my friend. That *es* before she takes over the hotel. Always she *es* asking questions about treasure.' Joe sighed. 'So many theories.'

'Like what, for instance?'

'Crazy *bruja*,' Joe's large eyes looked up at the nicotine-stained, cracked ceiling, 'She *es* convinced civilisation *es* brought to Mexico by the Egyptians when *es* the other way round.'

'That's *macho* Mexican bullshit, Joe.'

'No *toro* involved, my friend,' Joe smiled mysteriously. 'Something the archaeologists can never take into account, the time distortions of Eden.'

'Eden?' Double balked at the second mention of the word that day.

'Yes, *es* how America *es* before the Spanish,' Joe grinned. 'The garden where once grow the golden tomatoes of the sun.'

'Tomatoes?' Double chuckled. 'Don't you mean apples?'

'The tomato it comes from Mexico, and originally *es* golden, like the sun.'

'So they were described as apples, I can see that, but a garden? Come on, Joe.'

'*Es* an old legend my friend. Paradise before the serpent.'

'Yes, America *was* Arcadia and very likely it was visited by the ancient Greeks, and possibly other voyagers before them, hence the old story of the garden of the golden apples, I see that fits now, but time distortions?' Double frowned. 'How does that work?'

'Time flies when you are having fun, huh?'

'Always the way.'

'That *es* how it *es* in Eden,' Joe shrugged. 'A month there, a year any place else.'

'Uh, yea, right!' Double snorted.

'*Es* true!'

'You are asking me to believe that Mexican pyramids are older than the pyramids of Egypt?'

'*Si*,' Joe nodded slowly. '*Mucho*.'

'And Mexicans taught the Egyptians how to build them?'

'Those red-skins of the east have my esteemed ancestors, the master *borracho* builders, to thank for that,' Joe said with pride.

'What *borracho* builders?'

'*Es* a name we have for the pyramid builders,' Joe grinned. 'This tribe has a special liking for *mescal*, just the same as you.'

'And what about Moses, was he Mexican too?'

'By descent, yes.'

'And the pharaohs?'

'They are all *Mexicanos* up to the time of the Ptolemiys, when the line is broken and the ancient secrets lost.'

'As I remember,' Double said, picking his words carefully, 'The Ptolemlys invented map making as we know it.'

'*Si*,' Joe nodded. 'During that dynasty they were trying to recover the lost secrets from the Inkethatons, a dynasty very much into maps a long time before them, the most important of which *es* the location of the garden. Using a copy of one of these Inkethaton maps, Columbus sails to America, only in his map, the garden *es* called Atlantis.'

'My god.' Double slapped his head. 'Now I've heard it all,' he groaned.

'No, you have not.' Joe leaned closer. 'There is something more I must tell you.'

Menes, that was the pharaoh's name. The shrivelled daddy-mummy Helga had purchased from the Black Friars, recently reunited with his head, yet bereft of his penis, suited in conquistador armour back in the hotel, the source of all Double's sorrows apparently. Not his father exactly, save in a vague biblical sense, but his primogenitor nevertheless – multiply generations to the power of seven and you'll have the appropriate measure. Pull the other one, Joe, Double thought, wondering if the lost legacy from his father included his forefather's estate of the Americas. And, while you're at it, pour me another one, but this time make it a *mescal*, and have one on me too.

Siesta time, when even doppelganger dogs lie doggo, farting in stiff shadows. For once it was hot, no Englishmen about, nor Egyptians, or even pilgrims; only Double. One deranged survivor from a wreck of a life, staggering deserted streets, lost in a mangy dream.

This was himself, right? The one cardinal fact Double needed reminding of – shameless waster, for all that he was descended from a line of pharaohs and had a claim on the Americas, yea right, drunk in the afternoon, dragging his load past the soap-sud dome of the cathedral, bubble-brass doors barred against the sun and God and Jesus, cursed Shem-what's-its? This town in a state of perpetual denial, not even knowing its name. Like himself, Double reflected, taking a goat trail through scabby fields, gone hazy with heat, before reaching a high bluff commanding the desert plains thousands and thousands of feet below.

The world that existed elsewhere a riptide racing to the high heavens, the far mountains a bow aiming a quiver of arrows at the sky, so intensely blue his eyes hurt. Tears streaming as he stood bitten back by the savage *sierra* light, resisting what came next, delaying that moment, stretching it to infinity. Watching it winding a Möbius strip around the world, until, like a bat out of the blue, it hit him, shzam-bam, back of his head; that, if his existence as a thinking entity was measured by how he was always acted upon and rarely acted, he hardly measured up at all.

But like a glass that was half ... no, he corrected himself ... part empty, he was also part full. That elusive missing thought, notable by its absence, was therefore, in that sense, verifiable. Perhaps going towards explaining the gut feeling he had had ever since breakfast that morning, of being white bread with all the goodness taken out. The meat missing from his sandwich, the huff gone out his puff, the lead lost to his pencil when he was suckered into a game of blind man's bluff and misdirected by his reflection, nagual, essence, double's double, whatever it was, into swapping sides of a mirror simultaneously with a blinding flash – light from within *and* without, he realised, also experienced by his departing nagual – leaving him trapped here in Tláltipec, with all these dead ringers for characters he had known on the other side, inhabiting what he now thought of as the real world, instead of what it was, just another shadow play of old Lord Mictlántecuhtli in the Town With No Name, as he had come to call this place of ghosts, which he supposed he was numbered amongst. Scary thought, he was a spook like the rest, hanging on in Tláltipec.

The one exception being Joe, who, despite his evident and surprising lack of concern regarding Jaime, still seemed as substantial here as he was on the other side. However, even of Joe Double could not be sure, taking into account all the wormholes riddling the gorgonzola cheese of his memory. Starting with the mystery of what happened in the interregnum between escaping the fighting in Happy Valley and waking that morning back in his old room. His old room on the other side of a mirror, he reminded himself sternly, sure of nothing in Tláltipec any longer, and even whether he would find the hotel the same upon his return to face Helga; the harsh music of a counterpoint relationship in which he was not exactly sure who was haunting who.

4.   DOG COLLAR

That had to be a different hotel, Double told himself, staring up at an unfamiliar pink stucco frontage below a watchtower that hadn't been there before. Unless, of course, this was the same hotel pictured in the old sepia photograph hanging in a reception room, taken during the Cristeros insurgency of the 1930s. A trying time in the town, according to Helga, because it was then briefly occupied by the Cristeros themselves, who used the building as their HQ.

Yes, and there they were below, gathered around the open door, alive as anyone could be considering this was Tláltipec – the upper level of Mictlán, for the uninitiated – Cristeros choristers dressed for a sack-race, manic brothers and sisters, ash crosses dulling the raised foreheads of otherwise shining faces, *bandoleras* and rifles slung at cross purposes over shoulders, holding hands for holy joy, pogoing for Jesus, guns and revolution before barred Spanish windows under a flapping canvas banner proclaiming '*Vivo Cristo Rey*' in big red letters, bleeding on the wind.

'What the ...?' Words wrung out, Double getting his neglected thinking processes into gear, gawping as a broad-shouldered, imposing figure opposite – up to now with his back turned, conducting the heaven-facing choir, pocketing his baton in his Norfolk jacket and, turning, starting across the street towards Double, his jaw jutting under a thick head of tousled black hair, which brought to mind a typhoon on the loose.

'Who the ...? Double gasped.

'Who?' Reverend Who repeated, pushing head-buttingly close with flaring black eyebrows, seizing Double's hand in a vice-like grip. 'Names are not as important as what is in here,' he roared, knuckling Double's chest, his iron fist beating time to every word.

'Yea, right!' Doubled sniffed, reacting to a sudden guff of carbolic from the reverend's tweed jacket and matching britches. 'And they are?' he demanded, retreating a half-step, only just retrieving bruised fingers, nodding towards the choristers singing, '*Ay carramba, ave maria, hark hark the angelitos,*' or something like that. Straining to hear themselves over the snap and crack of canvas as, above, the banner stretched and slapped in the strengthening wind.

'*Los Cristeros!* Fighting for the soul of Mexico!' Reverend Who replied, closing the gap. 'You should join us, my brother. Become a foot soldier in the army of the lord!'

'Sounds challenging,' Double said, smiling down the gnashing assault of decayed teeth and staring eyes, seemingly smudged with coal, the eyelashes were so thick. 'Is there a war on?'

'Is there a war?' Reverend Who recycled. 'My God, do you not hear of the atheist hegemony? The communist plotters of Chapultepec?' he raved, peering psychotropically from behind the sluice gates of eyelashes.

'What the hell d'you think you're staring at?' Double snapped, taking another half-step back, wondering whether in his present white-bread, incorporeal, nagual-less state, he had anything left to protect.

'The mark of the beast, my brother. It is not yet upon you, but beware!' Reverend Who lofted a lightning-rod finger at the thunder clouds, stacking lead platters eight miles high over the gaunt buildings lining the narrow street. 'Lest it smite you unawares!'

'What beast might that be?' Double demanded, pressed with his back hard against cold stone.

'And it is written!' Again the Reverent lofted a finger, fairly sparking with messianic energy. '"Let him that hath understanding count the number of the beast! For it is the number of a man."'

'Yea, yea,' Double yawned deliberately, 'I know, *sex* and *sex* and *sex*. I've heard it all before, my man.' He thumbed towards the cathedral. 'I'm sure you have a lot in common with the Shemite Black Friars.'

'Shemites? Black Friars?' Reverend Who blinked, momentarily confused. 'I think not, those apostates are ... the ... corpse-eating communists of the antichrist!' he choked, bunching five in Double's face. 'We come to smite them!'

'Good man,' Double grinned, immensely cheered for reasons that eluded him. 'Perhaps I'll join you later, who knows?' he said, sidling away along the wall. 'But now, if you'll excuse me, Reverend Who.' He gave a mock bow. 'I have things to do.'

Helga? Double wondered, doubting the evidence of his eyes, suspiciously regarding a reception room, which, in his absence, had been converted to a hospital ward. The nurse was certainly broad enough, but humped like a bison? And dressed like that? The dowager of spades then, all black taffeta and bustle, except for thin wisps of silver hair straying her calico bonnet and straggling the white lace of her collar. Bent over the only patient in a delirium of agony, stretched out in the only occupied bed, in a far corner of the long room, where the upper walls and ceiling were striped black and tan by the swollen setting sun staring in through slatted shutters, reminding Double of the eye of a big cat, poised to pounce.

Helga the tigress? Or Grandma? he pondered. A far deadlier predator, if his father's one declaration on the subject was anything to go by. How had the old misogynist phrased it? Yes, the 'mother of harlots and abominations', somehow returned from the dead, posed as he always pictured her, furnishing his infant imagination with her scary stories at bedtime. When she said he had been *greedy*, about children buried alive in gingerbread mines. When she said he had been *irreverent*, about holy martyrs, boiled alive, burnt at the stake, eaten by lions, disembowelled, whatever. When she said he had been *bad*, about monstrous birds, usually the big black billed skuas that came swooping in the night and carried bad boys away, pinioned in their claws, to feed hungry chicks waiting in eyries high in witchy peaks above the clouds. Then, on rare days, when she said he'd been *good*, about treasure – all sorts: kings' ransoms, pirate hoards, Spanish bullion, sultans' gems, elfish silver, dwarfish gold, guarded by dragons, hidden deep within the mantled earth.

'There, there, that's better, isn't it?' she soothed in a crab-apple tone. Who else but Grandma, all bristles and barnacles, a face like the wreck of the Erebus, just as he remembered her through clearing mists of memory, bird billed and disdainful as ever, gimlet eyes fixed on his as, hesitantly, he approached her.

'Ah, there you are, *señor*,' she said, looking him up and down appraisingly as he came closer. 'Out walking again? Really,' she clucked, 'When a man in your condition should be resting.'

'And what condition is that?'

'Amnesia! You even forget your own name,' she sneered, ponderously turning her great bulk away as a piteous groan from the bed below drew her attention.

'Save me, sister,' the patient choked. 'They ... are coming!'

'And who the hell are *they?*' Double demanded angrily, wishing he had never gotten involved, looking down, wanting to look anywhere but the patient's horribly swollen face and his one remaining eye, next to a bloody socket that looked as though it had been pecked out.

'He means the Black Friars,' she said, nodding towards the hulk of the cathedral, imminent and transcendent through slatted shutters. 'The foolish boy thinks to run away from his duties at the cathedral.'

'What's his name ... sister?' Double said, almost calling her 'Grandma' in his confusion.

'What's *in* a name?' she said. 'When we are all sinners in the eyes of the Lord.' Pausing, she licked wrinkled lips with a purple tongue that was speckled orange and brown at the tip. 'Perhaps if you would be so good as to keep the poor boy company while I attend to my other duties,' she added, with surprising agility spinning on a heel and walking off rustling her bustle without another word.

'"Poor boy", did she say?' Double chuckled to himself, thinking the patient looked like more like a suffering Jesus on Nembutal, blood welling scratches on his forehead as if a crown of thorns had just been snatched from it, imploring him with black circlets, like coffee stains in a saucer ringing his one remaining eye, and the pain – the sweet, delirious pain – transmitted by tremulous fingers laid across the palm of Double's hand.

'What is that you say?' the patient rasped.

'So sorry,' Double said, his cheeks reddening with shame, realising he had been taking vicarious pleasure in the patient's pain. 'I was just mumbling to myself, honestly, that's all. Please don't worry, the nurse will be back soon.'

'The nurse! She is with them,' the patient croaked, flailing arms and rocking in the bed in a desperate bid to raise his wasted body.

'What, you mean the Cristeros?'

'Not them,' the patient mouthed, choking on phlegm and vomit. 'Though they are just as bad. I mean the apostates at the cathedral who deny the resurrection. To them, I am already dead,' he gasped, collapsing back on the bed. 'Is better you fuck me now. My superiors often use me that way. At least I will pleasure you with my dying breath, my brother.'

'You are perfectly safe with me,' Double said, wondering how to reassure him. 'I will protect you, I swear. No one will lay a hand on you.'

'My brother,' the patient said, suddenly calm, settling back onto sweat soaked pillows. 'Mark my words, before the dawn, when the crow caws thrice, you will betray me.'

'That's just the way it seems at the moment, my friend,' Double insisted, thinking this was a case of too much Bible study and not enough buggery. 'You must rest now.'

'No ... no...' the patient protested, struggling to sit up again. 'I have to tell you before they come ...'

Hell all the way back, and again, with suitable black magic rituals thrown in for good measure. In a nutshell, that was his story. How could Double believe him? It was simply too incredible that God-fearing Christians, apostates or otherwise could do what the Black Friars had. Trying him in a hastily convened ecclesiastical court. Draining his blood, sharing it in a ceremony that was a perversion of Holy Communion, leaving his insensible body staked out for the evil birds of the mountains. That detail, with its gruesome overtones of ritual sacrifice, Double found particularly horrifying, reminding him as it did of Grandma's warning of the awful fate waiting bad boys in the night. But he was regressing, this wasn't the nursery of his childhood, purple banded with her favourite bedtime stories. Once more the swollen sun was slipping past slatted shutters, but another place, another time. Not Double's story, but his friend's, the patient who had miraculously broken his bonds after night descended in the form of a pair of enveloping black wings and had his eye pecked out, then been chased by a monstrous bird, possessed of outsized claws – which presumably accounted for the razor-like slashes about his shoulders – and driven over a precipice into a ravine, where he was found by the town's goat herder.

And that dread secret, kept so long? Behind the Black Friars existed another order, a Masonic 'conclave', its purported purpose to protect Catholicism from corrupt elements within the church itself, as well as from the seductions of heathen religions, but perversely borrowing from both.

Thus do the gods reward puny mortals, Double reflected, his head reeling with the patient's ravings about obscure medieval orders on two continents, the Teutonic Templars, a secret society of shit-eaters. At the time of the supposed conquest, the society had for seventy years a toehold in the Americas. Its mission in the town, under the direct protection of the Aztec Eagle Knights, a cannibalistic martial cult, numbering among its initiates, a journeyman Teutonic Templar and Livonian knight. None other than the Hapsburg King of Spain, Carlos' protégé, Hernando Cortez, arch-kabbalist and co-conspirator, Wodenite and follower of Tezcatipoca, Lord of the Twenty Days, Shining Mirror of the Sun, still secretly worshipped in the mountains by the Black Friars.

Double would have learned more about this centuries-old corruption within the body of the church, had not Sister – Grandma – Helga, whoever she was, bustled in and shooed him out in a high-handed manner. His new-found friend's one eye followed Double accusingly as he slunk out the door, feeling he was betraying his trust somehow. But he was too weak to resist, or perhaps she was just too strong? Telling himself she couldn't remain at the bedside *all* night, Double resolved to return as soon as she left. But he failed to take into account her loud and wearisome prayers, addressed to the 'Lord of lords, in the highest of high' in shrill contralto hectometres that resonated the long corridors to his room, where he lay resting with one eye on the door, waiting for her to leave.

Cantina Joe, his face in a dream, looking in a door. No, not a dream. This was real, alright. Joe's real face then, looking in a real door. No, he thought, remembering he had gone through this before, not a door, a mirror that was a door! Come off it, Double groaned, reaching to the other side of the bed and pulling the other straw pillow over his head, just leave me alone and let me dream.

If only he could have admitted, at least to himself, he was just confused and needing help, lying there dozing, exhausted by all the goings-on.

'Wake up! Or you miss the moment, my friend!'

No time to consider what moment, or even which continuum. Joe, huge above, his boozy hooter hanging massive as a warty trunk. OK, so that was an exaggeration, but such was his mammoth effect. Behind him, spied as if through the wrong end of a telescope, bullfighting memorabilia on a far *cantina* wall, as Joe slowly faded from view and Double finally prised open gummy eyelids.

A dream, right. Yes, but in this town, Tláltipec was still the ongoing reality. Feeling chicken – and anything but brave – Double stumbled along the darkened corridor to the candlelit room, where Grandma de Farge was again on her knees, knitting wordy spells that, in his half-sleeping state, he perceived as ectoplasm entrapment crocheting a bed, and a substitute great-grandson who, as he was reminded by a line of song repeating his head, should have been him.

'I'm taking over,' Double announced with a determination contrary to the way he felt. 'You can go now, sister,' he said into her ear, kneeling down beside her. 'I'll take the next watch.'

No reply, unless he counted a low-brow Neanderthal frown he got in return. Perhaps she was weary and only just hanging on? No, not his *great-*grandma of the hump back, massive as a bison. How old? Around since that first cannibal feast. Cain her first son, and Able ... well, unable actually ... A strange conversation between the synapses of his brain while she recited prayers with an angry snarl.

'Great lord of days! We beseech thou, look down from thy smoking mirror amid thy astral armies of the stars. Yea, in thy infinite guiding wisdom, hear our humble prayer and accept the offering we bring, this poor repentant sinner, so weary of life, seeking succour and the shelter of thy encompassing wings ...'

'Sister!' Double interjected, sensing a rampant poltergeist of madness loose about the house, as the old sepia tinted picture of the hotel on the wall behind him crashed to the floor. 'You have to rest! Please allow me ...'

'And ... and ...' she gagged, dropping a stitch in time.

'Great spirit,' Double began mockingly, mimicking her pious tone, 'In your infinite mercy, look down on thy humble servant, so wracked and afflicted, a sinner, yes, but cheerful in the face of adversity, forthright in the defence of truth ...'

Now they were both going at it, her's the steel tongs and his the velvet hammer, their prayer marathon only just begun. No sense, apparently, making all the sense in the world to their patient, stirring into wraithlike life.

'My brother,' he managed, 'For fok's sake, shut the foking witch up!'

'I'm trying,' Double muttered, wondering what it was about the way the patient said 'foking' that chimed in his head.

But then the sister distracted him by redoubling her efforts, prayers flowing so fast the words blurred into one long gabble:

'And-consolation-in-your-bosom-in-accordance-with-thy-ineffeable-will-his-heart-and-his-gonads-redeemed-in-your-beninficense-salvation-his-sincere-desire-that-he-may-be-united-in-your-house-for-always-so-that-the-times-are-fulfilled-in-accordance-with-the-prophesies-of-your-servants-who-have-gone-before-glory-glory-faith-hope-and-glory-in-your-divine-malice-that-no-good-can-outwit-eternal-without-limit-sex-and-maximum-always-this-our-offering-o-great-one-humbly-we-pray-that-in-the-fullness-of-time-you-reach-down-and-pluck-the-unleavened-bread-of-our-offering.'

'Stop this unholy cant, sister!' Double shouted, jumping to his feet. 'You must leave, or ...'

'Or what, impotent pedant?' she raged, pushing her vastly greater bulk into his.

That was a mistake, physical intimidation invariably easier to handle than overweening sanctity, whatever the provenance. Invariably, all that is required is a modicum of resolution and a preparedness to strike first. As demonstrated by a lightning countermove - Double surprising even himself as conditioned reflexes born of Master Wu's martial arts weekend course at the local community centre near where he then lived came into play. Hitting her, just once, low in the pelvic regions, his rigid fingers sinking deep into Bible-black taffeta, shining the same blue sheen as Grandma's bilious bustle, his last sight every night in the nursery, as she leaned over to turn off the bedside light. Engulfing him in busty black folds, buttoned with bone cameos carved by Sami reindeer herders –miniature portraiture a local industry in Lapland apparently - into likenesses of his female forbears on the matrilineal side. Eidetically imprinting his retinas, as the electric element in the fly-speckled bulb hanging from the ceiling slowly faded and night invaded the nursery, with a ma, pa and grandma portrait parade, the three banes of his young life, alternating ad infinitum down the generations, pouring like pyroclasmic lava, replete with sounds and selective matrilineal and patrilineal memories, death and victory revisited, mud huts and granite piles, burying him until the first light of morning, and the first bird, tapping the nursery window.

All the above passed through his mind, as he stood, knees knocking with ebbing adrenaline and delayed action fear, reminded of a hooded crow, watching her hobbling away, cawing with thwarted rage and pain. Not the end of it, Double realised, knowing she'd be back, and with reinforcements. But at least he'd bought a little time to prepare a refuge for his new friend. The only place he could think of ...

Double was just wheeling the hospital bed into his old room, when the wardrobe door burst open and out swept three Black Friars. With their charcoal-smudged faces and hooded cassocks bringing to mind a hooded IRA death squad, their knotted hands swooped in a parody of the skuas of Double's childish nightmares.

Only then did the patient cry out, 'Do not forsake me again, my brother!' But, taken from behind, Double was unable to intervene, as, from the street outside, came a raucous cawing, just he was stuck a massive blow on the back of the head. A familiar portrait parade overwhelmed him as he fell.

5. BACK TO THE GARDEN

To some universes there are no open doors, the only way in by vaulting the journeyman's stile of the Tectonic third degree. In other words, over high enclosing walls – and those walls were higher than high – that blow to Double's head had sprung him back-flipping over the ramparts and into a garden, where nature was the gardener and the flower beds were unsullied by the hand of man. There, the dullest weed exceeded the rambling rose when it came to estimation of beauty or the efflorescence of their perfumes, and gorgeous plumed *quetzalcoatls* sang sweeter than any lyrebird, from tree canopies shading sun-dappled meadows watered by tinkling cascades, issuing crystal springs in three snow-capped mountains sloping down to a wide river flowing out to a cerulean sea and worlds beyond.

Too good to be true, Double's first thought, looking out from the grassy knoll where he had landed, reasoning there had to be a darker side to his surroundings, since, in the essence of all things, always lurks the opposite.

But at least he was *home*. Recognition slowly dawning as he followed a winding path through hummocky meadows, every footfall raising butterflies iridescent with every hue and colour, leading him in an enchanted cavalcade towards a high privet hedge, harbouring the mystery of concealing what lay beyond.

A palace, perchance? Crystal-paned windows overlooking a zoological garden where all the exotic species of this world were gathered? Perhaps a dusky sultan arrayed in silken robes encrusted with jewels, waiting in welcome by the gate? Yes, the idle fancies of a dreamer, carefree as a lark in summer.

No gate, just a leafy arch, an orchard beyond, trees heavy with golden fruit gleaming in the sun. This, he guessed, the fabled garden, rumours of which, like tap roots, had reached down the ages, feeding the imaginations of *sappatistas* and questers alike. Was it a dream? Yes, such a dream that only myths are made of – in eidetic vividness, surpassing the highest moments of Double's myth-spent youth, making everything else seem dull by comparison. Those golden apples, more than mere spheres, no less than solar orbs, radiant amid upper branches. Even to take bite would be sacrilege, Double thought, lost in wonderment, wandering leafy arbours, 'till at last he was called by a voice he remembered from before.

Recognising the cross-legged figure seated under a nearby tree, Double was overjoyed to see his one-eyed friend, cheeks round and rosy as pippins, glowing with inner light. Waving him over with an enthusiasm that seemed misplaced, considering the little assistance he had been when needed most.

'What is this place?' Double said, sitting down on the soft green sward of maidenhair grass beside him.

'It is the Eden under every sod. The sweetness at the heart of everything. It is everywhere, and at the same time nowhere, such is the parlous state of affairs between the foking worlds.'

'But what are *you* doing here?'

'I am the gardener.'

'Not the one-eyed king in the land of blind dreamers?'

Just the gardener.'

'So this isn't just a dream?'

'My brother, why ask when you already know the answer?' The gardener shook his head reprovingly. 'What little time we have is too precious to waste on idle questions. Even paradise has its snares,' he warned.

'Don't you mean snakes?'

'No, that would be to add to a Biblical misunderstanding begun in the Pentateuch by Shem and the patriarchs. The snake represents the royal road to wisdom. It is the energy that some call the kundalini, which in you lies sleeping, coiled at the base of the spine.'

'And the worm?' Double said, distracted by a leafy rustling above.

'Yes,' the gardener paused, looking up at a heavy black cloud sweeping in from the west, 'There is corruption even here. Not where you think.' Lowering his eyes, again he scrutinised Double's face. 'It comes with every new arrival.'

'You mean me, don't you?' Double protested, hot with shame, his heart jumping a beat. He could have hated his friend then.

'Of course,' the gardener sighed. 'But yours is a particularly bad case, *el gusano de diablo*. Don't you remember you swallow one whole?'

'In that *mescal*, Helga, or was it Grandma, gave me?'

The gardener nodded. 'Those entities are the double and the nagual of the being behind you,' he said, staring fixedly over Double's shoulder, his sunny face suddenly eclipsed.

No cloud that, Double realised, turning around, but the scything wings of an enormous black crow, swooping out of a perfect blue sky, spreading scimitar talons like some grotesque creature sprung from the Thousand and One Nights.

'No!' Double gasped, rooted to the spot by panic.

In that terrible first moment, his friend crying out, 'Help me, my brother, do not forsake me again.' His piteous plea, muffled as enormous black wings folded over.

What else could Double do, but turn and run – rent naked by abysmal fear, pursued by awful triumphalist cawing – into another dream?

No dream this, Double thought – would that it were – that old *bruja* spreading leviathan thighs, taking her time, and pleasure, lasciviously easing herself up and down, sucking his life force, her labia rough as sandpaper and dry as waterhole in a desert. A sudden flash of lightning outside, illuminating her face, leering ogerishly down over rustling black vestments, as the gasoline heat of her grindstone crotch transmitted a fever to his head.

'Get the fuck off and die!' Double spat, watching spittle splatter her nagual face, but there was no resisting the intense sensation washing over in waves, as, troll hands pressing on his, she held him down, pain and ecstasy like he'd never known, bursting an embolism in his brain.

But then, as her cardiovascular carpetbagger cunt contracted, he came and, simultaneously, an enormous detonation of thunder shattered roof tiles high above, a reflex action born of Master Wu's 'metal jacket' martial training came to his rescue, as he voided semen into his bladder, resultant kundalini energy surging to his aid, all the way from the chakra at the base of his spine to the crown of his head in that desperate moment as he made a desperate final bid to throw her off.

At last he was free, and Grandma Nagual was ... down, but not out, raising on hands and knees by the bed, and then she was up and running out the door, dragging her bustle, leaving a noxious odour as pervasive as rotten herring – a stain he knew would linger as long as the memory remained. Which, given his current condition, wasn't saying much, Double considered gloomily, staggering about, naked and disorientated by the stroboscopic flashes of lightning outside, fitfully illuminating the room as the storm passed over. He gathered up his clothes scattered about the floor, where his grandma had tossed them when he was out cold.

At last safe again in his room, Double was reaching out for a clear plastic envelope on the bedside table when, noticing movement at the corner of his eye, he looked round. Dead, I'm dead, he thought, on his first sight of the corpulent baron, obscenely dressed in body-hugging black battle fatigues. Standing where his reflection should have been, framed in the mirrored wardrobe door, stepping through, as Double stared, transfixed by shock, followed by three muscular monks in camouflage cassocks. The leading two, pointing semi-automatics at his chest, while the third, darting around, grabbed him by the arms and, cuffing his hands from behind, kneed him the small of his back, sending him stumbling into the open arms of the baron, greeting him like an old friend, planting slobbery kisses on his cheeks.

They were preparing to frog-march Double away when the baron, as if in afterthought, turned and booted the mirror through which they had just passed, smashing the glass into smithereens. Just one shard large enough remained for Double to make out a mirror version of the room with his insensible twin ... essence... nagual ... whatever, stretched out sleeping on the bed, before he was finally knocked out cold by a heavy blow to the back of his head.

6.   THE NAGUAL

Remembering nothing of a dream he had been sharing with his now insensible Double, a nagual awoke in the energy body they cohabited, like a couple of tourists caught in a mix-up over a time-share apartment built for one, only vacating it entirely for the other when lost in dreamless sleep. He opened his eyes, noticed a clear plastic envelope on the bedside table. Curious, he saw it contained a certificate granting him access to all areas of Mictlán. Assuming it was a practical joke in poor taste and not wishing to read more, he placed it back on the small table. Only then did he become aware of the wind rattling the window shutters, and a discordant choir wailing in the distance beyond. He could even make out some of the dirge they were so furiously singing: '*Ay carramba! Atender! Atender! Los heraldo angelitos cantar, Bless-ed be redeeming blood! Gory.(?) gory hal-le-lu-ja! Jésus es arrivé en Jerus-a-lem!*'

This, a nagual had to see. Precariously balanced on a wobbly old chair, standing on tiptoes, he forced open the shutters, almost falling out onto the street as he let in the gale. Hanging out, holding on with one hand, peering into the middle distance, he was just able to discern his friend Jaime, last seen in the *cantina*, starring in the cameo role of Jesus in the passion play. Missing an eye, it looked like, but of course that was his penchant for stage paint and over-dramatisation, his 'broken' body born up on a big wooden cross at the head of the procession, passing through the Plaza de la Revolucion about a quarter of a mile away. The wind bearing the stench of naphtha from a thousand flaring torches lighting the stone sides of the tumbledown medieval buildings lining the long street, dragging comet trails, lighting red the underbellies of monstrous clouds, scudding the sky above, reflecting on a many-headed beast below. The ecstatic faces of the crowd reminded him of gleaming scales on a side-winding snake, rippling with cohorts of red-crested helmets – Roman centurions lofting spears to the rhythms of thunderous drumming, shouting 'Hail!' and 'Hosanna!' and 'Smite the Egyptian hierophants!' – ascending the three hundred and sixty-five steps towards the cathedral and the Shemite soldiers of the antichrist preparing for Armageddon behind barred brass doors. Everyone playing the parts assigned them, this *que-loco* version of the passion. Over the top as was usual for *fiestas* in Mexico, confirming what the nagual had read about such occasions; the whole local community involved and playing it for real, in a drama where mayhem was guaranteed and absolutely anything could happen.

Suddenly, out of nowhere, or so it seemed, an enormous ungainly bird, black against flaring lights, slowly flapped across his vision, almost close enough to touch, cawing raucously. A bad sign, whatever it was, the nagual thought, dejectedly turning away and only then noticing the wardrobe mirror, now smashed in pieces on the stone floor. Seven years bad luck, he thought, but for who exactly? He hunkered down, picking up a piece, seeing his face and, over his shoulder, a figure standing close behind him.

'Shit!' he exclaimed, twisting round. There was no one, however, just his paranoid sense something heavy was about to happen. He had to get the hell out. But how and where, he wondered, with the town taken over by religious zealots, and harpy Helga and the evil Malinchés prowling the corridors beyond, preparing to ambush him before he made it to the front door?

Then he noticed, at the back of the open wardrobe, a low gap in the wall. Just like in Grandma's stories of castles and dungeons, a secret passage, leading who knew where? Perhaps this was what was meant by the 'privileged access to all areas' written on the certificate? Was Lord Mictlántecuhtli was clearing a way? he thought, threading the eye of the needle and squeezing through.

There *was* a pitched battle going on up there, he realised, the cavities of this subterranean world resonating with the distant din of fighting, and he wasn't playing his part. Lost without a candle in a labyrinth of narrowing tunnels, belly down, wriggling like the worm he was, when the earth beneath his hands heaved and the tunnel ahead caved in.

The nagual's first thought was of *sappatistas* at work at deeper levels, undermining the dimensions. His second, he was entombed, just as the certificate back in his room implied, trapped for all eternity in Mictlán, realm of the dead. But no, he realised, becoming aware of a glimmer of light from above as the dust began to settle. He was reminded that hope springs eternal. Hoping hope for an end to all this questing. He only ever wanted a better life, but something always took over, forcing him on. When, finally, he reached his goal, he felt small satisfaction at a road run, a puzzle solved, an answer found. The relief only temporary before, like a rat in a laboratory experiment, he would be given another electric jolt and forced into an untrammelled section of the maze.

There must be a genus of god-scientists, he reflected, devoted to the study of dyslexic life forms. Left or right? What's the difference when you have no choice but to go on and explore every rattrap hole presented. All down to the mutant questing gene, without which we would never have ventured far beyond the *kraal*, he guessed.

At least he could breathe easier here, no more belly wriggling in these chiselled colonnades; commodious corridors reverberating with sounds shafting ventilation pipes in the ceilings, spaced at regular intervals. And always it seemed aimed at the same luminary, the north star, he guessed, judging by the trajectory, the faint starlight – clearly visible once his eyes had adjusted – falling in ethereal blue pools on polished black onyx, reflecting haphazardly on silver veining, suggesting fire creatures climbing the walls. Quetzalcoatls or salamanders? Quetzalcoatls, he guessed. The fabled birds of paradise, dragging comet tails. Firebirds for the journey, marking his path with their finery. Secret signs or just natural formations in the rock? Hard to draw conclusions in that minimal light transmitted from the other side of the universe – the shafts acting like telescopes, separating and magnifying that one star from countless billions in the galaxy. A strange feeling, walking in the light of another sun. Relief really, as if, trapped as he was deep within the earth, he had also escaped planetary confines. Stella major acting on his brain, just as the spirit passages of the pyramids must have acted on Egyptian initiates into the great arcana in which, as Elias Levi wrote, all history, past, present and future, was writ in stone by the Nile. The nagual's mind was wandering. What had Egyptian pyramids got to do with Mexico? Everything, his twelfth sense told him. Yea, sure. But when he rounded that particular corner, all he saw was a dead end. If he knew something pertinent, why then the information so difficult to access? A function of his split-level brain, he guessed, those chiselled corridors, but one step up in the pyramid. And that was the connection, he realised. The cathedral above, like so many churches in Mexico, built on an ancient pyramid, and that only encasing an even older pyramid, just like the mid-brain is encased within the cerebellum, and that within the cerebrum. Each relating to a different age of man.

What walks on four feet, two feet, three, but the more feet, the weaker it be? The riddle of the Sphinx replaying in his mind, as he walked endless corridors that all seemed the same, threading the Cleopatra eye of that needle with the face of his mother – the eternal Helga – and the mummy of his ultimate forefather. Dead from thirst in the sands of Egypt. In a nagual, yet remembering. A cruel land. The unyielding sun, never setting, always stationary at high noon, until that final catastrophe when usurpers toppled his throne, casting him into the Well of the Worlds, leaving his son, the last of the line, walking deserted streets in a land with no name, towards his lawyer, for that final confession, when at last he would learn the terms of his father's will.

Thy will be done, thy kingdom come! But thy kingdom is blighted, the rivers run dry. And no fuel for fire. The forests all chopped down – just bitter cold of unyielding night, not even a star for company as he walked a hard road, questing ever westwards towards the setting sun, knowing his endless quest for a father's trust would soon be run. Love always denied, denied yet?

Then before him a great castle, flag-poled with towers to either side, a facade of pomp and misery, steps leading up to a rainforest atrium with mechanical cockatoos chirping and palm court musac playing – a commissionaire on hand to point him towards the offices across the steel and marble concourse – by glass doors, the partner's intagliate names illumined on a tablet of stone, Pagan, Crook and Crozier, waiting to take him down into the well of night, there to hear his sentence, he reflected, stopping by the reception desk, discovering he was early by a few minutes for an appointment he was unaware of having made, and the lawyer not at his post when the assistant rang through. Yea, he thought, take me down to the river, there to drink my fill of the black water. Piss and filth, swirling with blood of fatted calves. Yea, he resolved to drink his fill.

7.   THE EYE IS ON THE TABLE

How the minutes dragged, as the nagual looked for distractions in the foyer that could have been any corporate office, had it not been for the scattered mementoes of a Pickwickian past? Even in the matter of finding the right word, his amnesia played tricks on his mind. A polished oak stick rack and hat stand, three bronze busts of the founding partners – the original Pagan, Crook and Crozier – looking down on an arrangement of lilies in a Lalique glass vase on a round table of grey granite set before a reproduction Georgian fireplace. The new world from an old perspective, under the same guiding precepts.

The law is the law is the law. There shall be no greater truth than this; the received wisdom of Shem and the Patriarchs as laid down by Adam, in bound leather volumes, lining the book cases of a red-painted study that was the first circle of hell and the only warm room in the cold presbytery he knew as home, all of it coming back to the nagual now – amnesia no defence in Tláltipec any more – remembering the great man, pre-heating a son's young bottom before the roaring gas fire, bending him over his knee, announcing solemnly, 'This is going to hurt me far more than you. Never question my orders, and that is an order! Only after you have proved your obedience, submitting to my will in all matters, will you be allowed that privilege, young master.' Then the whacks raining down on his padded behind, his pants packed with pages torn from the encyclopaedia.

'Amen to artillery.' He was a sapper, even in that remote past, before he was boarded out to Elias Asshole's Reformatory for Wayward Boys, then cast out for undermining imposed reality and questioning orders. His father's image clouding over in the years that followed, moribund in memory banks, a grey headland socketed like a skull, looming over the fogs and a cold sea. As he imagined, alone in his school dorm, boarded out even in the summer holidays. Baffin Island, or somewhere like that beyond the Arctic Circle, unvisited since Frobisher's expedition seeking the fabled north-west passage to India, home to colonies of shrieking skuas and fulminating fulmars, his whetstone visage crumbling as a cliff undermined by time and tide – the changing mores of a tide-race century. But always in the roar of those breakers, the nagual could hear the pounding beat of his father's words – a coda more binding than the precepts of the elders of Zion and the Pentateuch, the first five books of the Old Testament, or, as the pedant preferred to call them, 'The 'Recension of the Babylonian Talmudists'. His stentorian ringing tones, carrying even through the door of the great study, closed on the regular Saturday matinee sessions, which always continued to the small hours of Sunday. When the conclave of elders convened to discuss the minutiae of the Bible, or so he once coldly informed him, after a sermon on minding his own business – lords of the cloth, monsignors, bishops, professors of moral logic, judges, historians and theologians – layman's opinion usually represented by his sometime shadow and advisor on temporal affairs, Mr Crook ...

Shuffling arthritically past, his father's loyal servant; could that *really* be him? Clutching a familiar-looking cracked black leather portmanteau to his preposterous pinstripe Saville Row front, myopically peering about over half-moon gold spectacles, across by the reception desk? Some things might have changed, such as these offices, but Mr Crook never, the nagual considered, inwardly flinching – expecting a knuckle-grinding crunch as the last time – but meeting no resistance as they shook hands.

'Ah, the young master,' he croaked, peering owlishly over thick lenses. 'Can it really be you?'

'*Yes, in the flesh! Sprung out of a dream ... My father's dream of a son and successor, dashed on the black rocks of a north-western promontory,*' the nagual wanted to say, but instead merely mumbled, 'Mr Crook, so good to see you. How long has it been?'

'More years than I'd care to count, young master,' the old lawyer said, joints creaking like rusty hinges, leading the nagual down red carpeted stairs to the basements, holding open the door to an anonymous office suite that smelt of cleaning chemicals, with dusty ledgers crowding metal shelves.

'Sit yourself down, young master,' he went on, indicating one of two plastic chairs and taking the other, setting the portmanteau on the table between them. 'An onerous duty, and not one I confess I have been looking forwards to over much.' Sighing, he reached into the portmanteau, setting a sheaf of documents on the table like Doc Watson spreading a hand of cards. 'Your father was certainly not the most receptive man in the world when it came to taking advice.' He paused meaningfully. 'And let me tell you, on more than one occasion, I tried to dissuade him against drafting this will. But, as you know, when he made his mind up on something, your father was impossible to budge.'

Even though such a detail measured the limits of his knowledge of his father, the nagual nodded – an old curmudgeon to friend and foe alike, this much he had already gleaned. 'Is there a problem with the will?' he asked after a judicious pause.

'Yes,' Mr Crook nodded slowly, 'I should say there is, young master. You see, your father employed an arcane legal device that went out of use in the eighteenth century.'

'That figures,' the nagual grinned. 'Behind the times as always, my antediluvian old man.'

Ignoring what he obviously considered a distasteful witticism, Mr Crook continued briskly, 'You needn't worry with the legal terminology but, suffice to say, the effect was to create two back-to-back wills.'

'So there's two wills?' the nagual gasped.

'If you think of it that way, it will help you understand what control over the destiny of his children your father retains.'

'Retains?' the nagual reiterated. 'You talk as if my father is still alive.'

'Would that he were, young master. Would that he were,' Mr Crook said heavily, regarding his client gravely over half-moon spectacles, 'Then at least I would be spared this onerous task.'

'And who are these other children?' the nagual insisted, ignoring the lawyer's pained look. 'Did he marry a second time?'

'You *really* don't know?' Mr Crook's eyes narrowed. 'Even aware as I am of your father's capacity for secrecy, I find that incredible.' The lawyer sighed. 'After you were packed off to that school, the woman I always knew as the housekeeper, I am referring of course, to your mother,' he smiled opaquely, 'Had triplets. Three baby girls, identical in every respect. It was the sensation of the parish, the one dark blot, or perhaps I should say three,' he made a strange gurgling sound, 'In your father's forty years ministering to the needs of his flock.'

'And what do they look like, my sisters?'

Tugging his right ear, Mr Crook further distended a pendulous lobe. 'I was never very good at this but I will attempt a description,' he said, clearing his throat. 'Like your father, I would suppose, the same black hair and handsome dark eyes. But I have not seen them since they were babies, after the housekeeper... ah ...' He gave his secret smile again. 'Your mother left.'

'Do they know about the will?'

'I should say they do,' Mr Crook nodded. 'They have an appointment at the end of the week, and I don't consider it breaking a confidence to tell you, I shall probably be offering them the same advise as you.'

'Which is?' the nagual snapped, aware that the lawyer had just overstepped the bounds of probity into that no-man's-land under vulture-high command, where self-interest is the one pertinent law.

'You should think long and hard before submitting to the terms of your father's will,' Mr Crook said carefully. 'Quite apart from the first problem I mentioned, he has employed a number of other codicils to create a series of interlocking trusts, administering the component parts of his estate. Variously stocks and bonds, lands and other holdings, moveable assets and life assurance policies ...'

'And what is the point of all this?'

'I believe his intention was to place your mother in a position of absolute power, at the same time enmeshing her in an irreversible process not of her design. She is chief executrix, heading each of the trusts, and though your sisters are required to serve in a lesser capacity, collectively they can never muster enough votes to challenge her position.'

'And my role in his game plan?'

'Only that of powerless onlooker, I am afraid. For reasons known only to himself, your father chose to exclude you from serving in any capacity on the various trusts.' Mr Crook frowned. 'What was it your father said when we discussed all this? Ah yes,' he muttered, '"Fate or destiny? How will my boy decide?" I never did understand what he meant by that. Unless of course he was referring to the island of your mother's birth.'

'Do you know the name of it?'

'Unfortunately not,' Mr Crook inclined his head, 'However I do know it is one of three mountainous islands, located exactly on the Arctic Circle.'

'Yes, I heard that.'

'Your father said the fact was most significant.'

'Do you happen to know why?'

'I am sorry to say I do not, young master.' Mr Crook shook his head.

'Perhaps places, just like people, have their doubles, and those islands have their counterparts, too. Say, three mountains on the tropics? Do you think that is possible?'

'I am afraid you have lost me, young master,' Mr Crook said condescendingly.

'Never mind,' the Nagual snapped. 'What else do you know about the islands?'

'Only that they are near the, ah, Saltstraümen.'

'What's that exactly?'

'A whirlpool, the largest in the world, I believe, located somewhere off the north coast of Norway.'

'So it's confirmed, my mother's Norwegian, yes?'

'You may be correct young master, however your father never discussed her nationality, so I cannot say.' Mr Crook paused. 'As regards the island, all I am reasonably sure of, it is one of three within the tide race of said whirlpool on the Arctic Circle and there is a most curious phenomena associated with them, which of course your father was fascinated by.'

'Of course,' the nagual groaned, wondering how much more he could take.

'Your father was interested in anything that seemed to defy the normal bounds of time and space,' Mr Crook said.

'And these islands do that?'

'It would seem so, young master.' Mr Crook nodded, unperturbed. 'Your father mentioned that the

Elizabethan explorers referred to them as floating islands, and I believe since time immemorial sailors in those parts have called the associated spectre the "Fata Morgana".'

'I think I heard of that,' the nagual sighed, wondering where and when. 'It's some sort of mirage, right?'

'A superior mirage, young master. Stretching and twisting the islands into fantastical forms that your father ascribed to the Möbius effect, as he called it.'

'I don't understand.'

'Frankly neither do I, young master. However, I did gather that, when the whirlpool appears in the mirages, some very strange effects can take place.'

'Such as?'

'I am afraid there I would be drawn into the realm of the purely speculative, something, as a lawyer, I cannot allow,' Mr Crook smiled lopsidedly. 'However, I'd hazard a guess that your father told you about the spectre when you were a boy. It was one of his best stories, Perhaps you've forgotten?'

'No, I don't think so,' the Nagual said firmly.

'Be that as it may, your father was quite illuminating on the subject. As I recall he said that the phenomena was caused by the interface between warm air resting on a layer of colder air immediately above the ocean, creating a refracting lens over which distant objects on the horizon appear to hover, projecting the apparition to diverse places.'

'Such as Mexico, I suppose.'

'Mexico?' Mr Crook said blankly.

'I was thinking of my mother's habit of appearing when not wanted.'

'Ah, I see,' Mr Crook gurgled. 'You were making a joke.'

'Correct,' the nagual grimaced. 'Look, all I want to know is what is the upshot of this ...' he paused, searching for an appropriate phrase, 'Bagatelle of shit.'

Mr Crook winced. 'You are referring to your father's estate?'

'Of course,' the nagual nodded.

Mr Crook sighed. 'I'll attempt to summarise. Your mother has a life-rent over all properties, land and holdings, moveable assets, stocks and investments, until she dies. And when that day comes, if there is anything left, which, knowing your mother and her spendthrift ways,' he coughed, discretely covering his mouth with a fly-blown parchment hand, 'I rather doubt, then the second will comes into operation, creating another tier of trusts and, at the head, a daughter of her choosing, the purpose of which will be to dispose of all remaining moneys to the surviving issue, including yourself should you live that long.'

'And *you* rate that an unlikely prospect?' the nagual glowered.

'Not at all, young master. Quite to the contrary in fact. From the little I learned from your dear father on the subject of his housekeeper, your, ah, mother, I understand she comes from an extremely long-lived line, and you can count at least one centenarian on the, ah., Lapland side of your family. So it is just that you may have to wait a rather long time for your inheritance.'

'I see,' the nagual said heavily. 'So you think I shouldn't have any part of it?'

'You should consult with another lawyer before you make up your mind, but, yes, that is my considered opinion.' He nodded sagely.

'But what's the point when I get nothing if I do?'

Mr Crook shook his head. 'In that event your dear father left a locked box, which I have secure upstairs at reception, should you wish to make that choice.'

'And what's in this box?'

'That I cannot say, young master.'

'Can't or won't?'

'Your dear father did not see fit to tell me.'

'Well, is it heavy, for example?'

'For a small box, I suppose you might say it is.'

'Heavy enough to contain gold, for example?' the nagual interjected hopefully.

'Possibly, but personally I rather doubt it.' Mr Crook shook his head. 'Your father always placed a greater faith in redeemable government bonds. Gold, he would say, is merely the stock in trade of pawnbrokers and jobbing jewellers.'

'Am I allowed to open this box before I decide?'

'No, I'm afraid not. Your dear father was most specific in his instructions, but knowing him as I did, and how often he spoke of his great love for you, I suspect it contains something of worth, perhaps even of inestimable value.'

'You are sure about that?'

'Your father would not leave you destitute, of that I am absolutely certain, young master.' Mr Crook smiled, exposing yellowed dentures. Death looked the nagual in the face at that moment. How could he have known his father's lawyer was numbered among the living dead. Not a legal eagle exactly, more a pin-striped vulture, grown rich from advising widows and orphans, picking over the spoils of victory in a no-man's-land on the dark side of Tláltipec.

Putting aside his paranoia of lawyers, the nagual took his time making up his nagual's mind. Left alone in that airless room, pouring over the poorly Photostatted document that seemed an insult in itself, the print smudging under his fingers, the right margins borrowing a strip from each following page, grappling with arcane legal gobbledygook terms such as 'without prejudice, per stripes, the said residue' and 'residue of that residue, renunciation, forgoing purposes, parameter powers, hereunder, aforesaid, intestacy' and 'immunities' – Cronus' revenge implicit in every line – his father's will suborning him to submit and watch from the side-lines as his share was frittered away, and yet, his father's flunky assured him, the great man had greatly loved him. What to do with that pathetic love that could ignore him so resolutely? But perhaps his father was merely following a hallowed family tradition. So who then to blame? His father, or his father? A stain of Biblical proportions extending to the seventh generation? Seven to the power of seven more like, he considered, remembering a pyroclasmic portrait parade of simulacrum, simian ancestors, scrolling by. Overwhelming him, every night as he passed into sleep in the nursery – how many years ago? All the way back to the deluge and before, to that founding father who first pissed in his genetic soup, that proto-ancestor, the veritable worm at the roots of his family tree. Within him yet, an ancient Egyptian of some rank he had little doubt, given his father's predilection for pomposity and Pentateuch studies. But perhaps he was just inventing scapegoats. Maybe he'd rejected his father's love in a past too distant to remember, and this was all his fault. There is no refuge from guilt, even in infancy. From birth we are all answerable, he thought, and only behind the closed doors of death is judgement pronounced.

But at least he'd learned a few notable facts. According to Mr Crook, the housekeeper, his father's nemesis, came not from an island associated with a mirage called the Fata Morgana, located near the cauldron of the Norns, reputedly the largest whirlpool in the world, somewhere off the north coast of Norway. While just as weirdly, his father had been born to unnamed Coptic parents at the turn of the century and was fostered by Catholic nuns at the Sacred Heart Orphanage in Alexandria, Egypt; all this recorded in a legacy of seventeen thousand dollars to the order. A snip against the value of the estate, but, as off-shore accounts were still being uncovered by the diligent Mr Crook, and there was ongoing litigation with the Egyptian government for compensation for lands nationalised during the Suez crisis, that amount had yet to be determined.

Fate or destiny? The same riddle he'd posed his father, merely by existing, returned from beyond the grave via his chosen mouthpiece, Mr Crook. But didn't both words mean the same thing? A dictionary on hand on an upper shelf provided the answer. Fate, in the original sense, was the sentence pronounced over the birth of each individual by the original three weird sisters, known as the Norns, by his long-lived Laplander forebears on his mother's side, and accepting it meant accepting one's lot – in this case, he supposed, submitting to the provisions of his father's will, just as he supposed his father had all those years ago, when trouble arrived in his life in the form of Helga. But destiny – implicit in the notion of the 'quest' and deriving from the Latin root *'destinatus'* – was subtly different, meaning the end or ultimate purpose for which an individual had been incarnated, and every life was a chance to achieve it. Knowing that, and notwithstanding his suspicions of Mr Crook, he really had no choice but to pick up the gauntlet, take the box and unlock the riddle which destiny had posed him.

'*My father, wherever thou art, whether in heaven or hell, hallowed be thy name, thy kingdom come, thy will be done ...*'

Murmuring this as an incantation against any time-locked Jacks or Djinns, the nagual resisted the temptation to call his father 'shit-eater' and say, 'cursed be thy name, thy kingdom be undone', so much did he hate him then. His father, whose gold he lusted after as a desert hawk seeks the sun, Horus soaring on thermals flying into the face of Ra, in his quest for that eternal love, laying the cold metal box on reception desk, inserting the key, holding his breath for fear of the unknown. Telling himself what will be will be – wondering whether he'd regret his choice – turning the lock, lifting the lid, revealing a book bound in yellow hide, branded on the bottom left hand corner a portion of a circled cross, or perhaps a claw? The nagual wondered, imagining his father in Bedouin robes, like Abraham in the Bible, two hands raising a knife high, about to sacrifice the original fatted calf – his beloved son, Abel, bound and disabled, laid out on a stone altar at the behest of an angry God.

Dismissing the notion as too fantastical, even for him, the nagual turned the tanned skin cover, and the red and black marbled fly leaf to the Latin-dated title page, reading out loud:

'*The Book of Tell-Tale Signs, Volume One.* Is this all I get?' The nagual's soaring hopes plunged to earth, hawk wings singed by the solar disc. 'Where are the other volumes?' he demanded, tasting bitter defeat at that the moment.

'There is only one volume, and you are holding it,' Mr Crook sighed over his shoulder. 'The great project to which he devoted more than half his life. Perhaps it was his wish you should complete it. Now that would be a *worthy* task.'

'Fuck that for an epitaph,' the nagual snorted, flicking the pages, watching a fly-past of hand-drawn signs, some of the images rudimentary – almost childlike in conception, caricatures of animals and plants rendered like hieroglyphics, others exceedingly complicated, reminding him of computer circuitry and squiggly sequences of DNA. 'This is of no value whatsoever,' he declared.

'Perhaps not of financial value, young master,' Mr Crook murmured, 'But your father's scholarship was unequalled in his chosen field of study.'

'And what was that?' the nagual demanded, the rage he felt inside a molten riptide of lava.

'Why, I am astonished you do not know, young master! Your father was perhaps the greatest kabbalist of his age.'

'Kabbalist?' The nagual frowned, fearing his worst suspicions were about to be confirmed. 'Do you mean my father was into black magic? Is that how he made his money?'

'Not at all, young master, not at all,' Mr Crook said reassuringly. 'Your father was a reverend, a God-fearing man who made his money by scrupulous share dealings, I can assure you. If he did gain some small advantage from his knowledge of the Kabbala, which he once told me in Hebrew means "received love", it was no more than he deserved.'

'But what use is this to me?' the nagual moaned, noting, as he flicked over the remaining pages, a change to runic symbols. 'There's no text.' He made a fist. 'Not one damned word of explanation.'

'I really do not know, young master. Perhaps if you peruse the book closer you will find out,' the lawyer declared airily, pulling out a gold fob watch and chain from a pocket of his old-fashioned waistcoat. 'Good heavens,' he babbled, peering at the moon-phase enamelled face, 'I had no idea it was so blessed late. Please forgive me, I really must fly.'

8. BACK ON THE GOLF COURSE OF LIFE

More satanic transformations, the nagual considered sourly, regarding Beelzebub pinstripes of the parasitic variety, buzzing off and out the glass double doors. Drawn by the dung of another death, perhaps? The ordure of pastures new? Time to pack up and go, he thought, holding the book to his chest, but where? When he was stuck between the continuums, with no place to call home? But then, just as he turned back for the box, still open on the reception desk, his grip on the book loosened and something slipped out and fell to the floor. An old monochrome postcard, he saw, stooping to pick it up, presenting the pictorial map of an instantly familiar skyline of witchy peaks. Yes, the three sisters in jagged relief, from more or less the same perspective as he first remembered seeing from the bus, but somehow removed from bandit foothills and set down in a cold and comfortless sea. A prospect only somewhat softened by snow-capped summits, wreathed in spiralling mist, tall pines clinging to precipitous rock faces tumbling down to lower slopes, with meadows and patchwork fields dotted by hut settlements and grazing longhorn cattle, their shaggy brown coats rendered in exquisite detail. Boiling surf directly below, where running cliffs brimmed a monster whirlpool, named not Saltstraümen, as Mr Crook would have it, but, according to the card, the 'Cauldron of the Norns'. A scene, perhaps captured in a witch's eye, mirrored in a fish lens as she poured over her Norn's scrying glass. The monster whorls of that maelstrom rippled every which way, making it look as if the rugged islands that were all that prevented the ringing horizon and the world beyond from being sucked into the maw of the deep and torn to pieces by flotsam teeth, flossed by sails and rigging of all the sailing ships that had passed that way before.

Down the plughole, into the Well of the Worlds, that was for sure, the nagual reflected, a fleeting mental image replacing the panorama on the card, with thundering falls cascading in infinite cupcake gradations into a raging sphincter he knew he had once rimmed himself, chancing his way out of the abyss in Mictlán, the domain of the dead, he suddenly recalled.

Repressing a shudder, he turned the card over in his hand and smiled, a sudden flush suffusing his normally pallid features, as though his cheeks were brushed by an unseen hand. The nagual saw it was addressed in his father's characteristic crabby handwriting to the 'Young Master at the Presbytery'. His pleasure diminished, as he noted than it had obviously never been sent, for there was no stamp or postmark.

'My *dear son*,' it began,

'*This is a map of the Islands of the Elect, which you will not find in any atlas since they exist only in the minds of poets and dreamers. In the ancient myths they were always located at the very limits of the world. One day I hope to meet you there.*

Till then, when we renew our acquaintanceship,

with very much love, your father xxx

P.S. Perhaps the other enclosure I have included will assist you on your quest.'

Did the nagual hear echoing laughter as he read this? Those 'Islands of the Elect' marking the place of his exile, in heaven or perhaps hell. A mirage, screened offstage in the abyssal black depths of a monster maelstrom that, on the flimsy evidence of the card, if it existed at all, was called the Cauldron of the Norns, sucking all the way to Mictlán for all he knew, out of sight but not out of mind behind the enclosing *tzitzimime* wings of the lord of death. And that enclosure mentioned so casually? Another map interleaved between pages of this *fabulous* inheritance, he thought bitterly, reflecting that it was all he had got in the way of 'received love' from his double-dealing kabbalistic father. Something about the map was familiar, yet unlike any he could recall. Desiccated by age, yet preserved in livid colour, the pigments unfaded by time, showing crudely drawn coastlines dotted by tracks and odd, symbolic-looking squiggles resembling cuneiform script, suggesting perhaps place names and significant points, described in code.

Perhaps the puzzle of the indexed landmarks had kick-started the old sod's interest in the Kabbala? the nagual pondered. A memory returning of a hobgoblin face, peeking in his bedroom door, seen prismatically through eyelashes as he lay snoring artfully in the way of kiddies feigning sleep. Watching his father tiptoeing in, then standing, staring down, breathing hard through a military moustache, before reaching towards the shelf behind the young master's head. What had he been up to so furtively? Was theft on his mind, or had he been clutching something when he leant over? Picturing his attic room as it then was, the legend 'Beware of Rufus the Dog' warning intruders in suitably toothy black lettering painted on knotty wood, the varnish stained and yellow with age; beyond the door, his sagging collections weighting chipboard shelves, treasure discovered during long country rambles that took him deep into the jungles of Chichen Itza, detouring with his penknife machete through the bramble thickets of Michoacan, before returning with pockets full of artefacts to record and catalogue in his museum of lost civilisations. The shiny dragon's tooth, found in the furrows after the spring planting, evidence of a former age of Titans, when giants ruled the earth; shards of pottery brought by travellers from far-off countries, the nagual could still see like enchanted islands in his mind's eye, empires and principalities once ruled by impressive names such as Prester John, Tamerlane and Montezuma; shells and bones of prehistoric fish – the skeleton of a coelacanth discovered outside the fishmonger's, confirming the Biblical story of the flood. Cast-off carapaces of crawlers yet unknown to botanists; rusty bottle tops left in the beech woods from bacchanalian orgies before the time of Christ; each item proving the world was far more incredible than the planet-wide prison of proscriptions his father, with all his strictures and pronouncements, had insisted it was, as he now seemed to recall.

Was he wrong? Did his memory lie? No! Twice no, the nagual told himself, suddenly becoming aware of an overhead CCTV camera monitoring his movements. Making that his cue, running out of claustrophobia-conditioned offices into the atrium past the commissionaire and his shiny row of medals, taking the steps to the street three at a time, hitting on smoggy rush-hour air, realising this was Manhattan on a wet Friday winter's evening, the lights all at red and the traffic backed up a zillion blocks, all the way over the Hudson to the new territories in China. Lost for direction – checking the map for curiosity's sake, finding a little symbol of a castle with scales placed to the side, a dotted line at a tangent, suggesting left, left, then dead ahead.

Directions the nagual felt bound to follow. And, sure enough, after a couple of turns, arriving on a broad and empty highway, with easy walking on ample grass verges.

He had reached that border between one fiction and another, where suburbs give way to abandoned industrial estates, pylons leaking radon over dog kennel factories sitting not so pretty amid acres of cactus-cracked concrete, corrugated asbestos, sagging under the accumulations of loam and leaves. All this propped against the backdrop of the city. Shanghai? He guessed it could be. Pagoda high rises all lit up with dancing paper lanterns, brightening as darkness slowly fell ...

And ahead? Like the lost enchanted islands of his childhood, featherbedded on murky patchwork depths, the purple hills of the Southern Uplands, rearing over scattered clumps of trees, marooned in mist, calling him from unfenced heather vastness to venture yet further into the rippling blue yonder where the world whorled away over the purple banded horizon, and into the high chaparral of his boyhood badland dreams, where three witchy peaks cowled in snow looked down on picture-book revolutionaries riding shotgun on hijacked trains, trailing steam across the tarbrush *mesas* dotted with the fires of bandit encampments, past sombreroed Indians laying in ambush for passing *gringos*, hiding behind desert bluffs spiky with cactus.

Night, and no hayrick to lay his head, not even a rock to afford shelter from the bitter wind. Was this his sentence? To be a vagabond between the dimensions, a wraith glimpsed between blinks by commuters, sailing past on interstate flyovers, cruising en route home from the office or wherever they worked, orbiting the whorls of a witches eye. A scene caught in a fish lens, each one aloof behind bubble-tinted glass in their bloated chariots puffed out with self-importance, secure with index-linked pensions, gazes fixed on geriatric condominium, glittering in the setting sun, dipping over cancerous city conurbations eating up the worlds. His lot, hunger and hopelessness, facing an uncertain destiny. Questing as long as there was life in these old bones. Old? Somehow age had crept on him unawares. His golden youth gone like so many golden coins scattering into the dark gully below, lost under heavy clouds when he turned to look. Nothing else to do but push on into the biting wind towards the rugged summits, at last to find a lookout point where he might contemplate all this.

But then a hole got in the way, a gusset parting in the heather and he was down - screw-balling zinc-shoed darkness, only just escaping the cut with another low score marked on his card. An eagle birdie at the ninth, actually a hole-in-one, since, from tee to green under the Town With No Name and taking in New York and

Shanghai, was a par three. All detailed on a map with distances and dangers to avoid. Bunkers wide enough to lose the Sahara in, rough where it was advisable to go armed with something sharper than a no. 3 Panga iron, and one was in as much danger from stampeding elephants as from roaming bands of Masai speculators. Yes, the golf course of life, where the general aim is to extend your handicap and take as many shots as possible to get round. Just a few make it over the hundred.

Strangely, the hole only got deeper as the nagual descended, tumbling time into a new game – another life, he supposed, wondering what face would next be stitched onto his – as he was sucked into wormhole rapids stretching with chewing gum faces; cross-wielding Cristeros battering it out with bludgeon-battling Black Friars. This was the nagual's final sight as he was enveloped in the dust and hail, finally landing with a thud that clean knocked the breath out of him, back to the ground, staring up at black-brassiered ridges crosshatched by lightning striking out of a clear blue sky, and the lazy circle formed by three flail-winged raptors, gyring on a tornado twisting away in the distance, reminding him of that fateful glass of *mescal* and a *pocito* gut-wriggler – *el gusano de diablo* – doing the *sombrero samba* just the same.

But then a jackboot blocked his view, so highly polished he could see his face reflected – well, he guessed it had to be his – proximity to gloss brown leather making it a near certainty. Old? Yes, indeed, enough lines to map Antarctica, worm tracks charting a course almost run. Death sunny side up, clawed by crow's feet.

'We leave this *chinga* for the vultures!' announced a *castiliano*-accented voice over a distant fusillade of gunshots. 'What you say, *el capitán*?'

Now there were two pairs of jackboots blocking his view, razor-billed officers of the Cúerpo del Cuervo Négro, the 'black crow brigade', in stylish jodhpurs and belted battle fatigues. The officer who was rhythmically slapping a swagger stick against his palm, the nagual guessed was *el capitán*, shaking his capped head, the shiny brim resembling a gleaming black beak from that low angle.

'No, I think not! There is life in the old wretch yet. And who knows, maybe he is the one?' Raising a hand, he snapped fingers to a medical orderly, stepping up to his command. 'Gustavo,' he snarled, 'Strip and search the prisoner. Same drill as the others, an enema and a diuretic. After you have checked his vomit, take him away for interrogation.'

105

9.   THE TORTURER

Meat markets were like this, the nagual considered, taking in his surroundings in covert little glances, carcasses arranged for inspection, spread-eagled on slabs, hooked and racked like so many unbuttoned coats exposing what every medical student is required to know, the floors swilling with blood and puke. All around men screaming for mothers, Madonna and mercy; God and Jesus, fourth and fifth in the pecking order respectively. While black-hooded *torturadores* moved from table to rack and back again, using body concavities for ashtrays, applying *bastinos*, adjusting thumbscrews, garrottes, gouging gonads, scrying entrails for clues. From what he could gather, all because of a map someone was holding.

That someone was him.

'*Oye, campesino!*' a voice rang out over the hubbub, addressing him from the next table. 'I hear say you are the *one?*'

'*¿Estás loco?* An old man like me!' the nagual laughed bitterly, making a pretence of struggling against his bindings – in any case so tight he could barely move his head, let alone arms and legs. 'Only young men have that sort of luck!'

'There is no luck in this place, just pain,' the anonymous voice insisted. 'I think you are lying, old man.'

'Yes, I am lying, lying on my back, owning nothing but my nakedness,' the nagual cackled, 'And soon to be dead, for which I thank the godness of good!'

'You are sure about that?'

'Of good no! His godness? Never! But of death, yes! Lord Mictlán is close you know, I saw him, with my own eyes, before they brought me here.'

'And what does Lord Mictlán look like, old man?' the anonymous voice retorted scornfully.

'Like a black crow with the sky in his shiny beak, my son. The soldiers call him *el capitán*.'

'*El capitán del garra!*' the anonymous voice rejoindered tartly, his manner leading the nagual to suspect he was a schoolmaster. 'But only behind his back,' he added warningly.

'Why do they call him "the claw"?'

'Because he is the tool of the abomination that lives in Chapultepec!'

'Chapultepec?' the nagual croaked back. 'I know this name, but for the life of me yet remaining, I cannot remember from where.'

'Don't you know Chapultepec *es el* Castillo del Presidenté in México City?'

'Is it far *estas castillo?*' the nagual asked, knowing ignorance was his best cover.

'My god!' the voice moaned oratorically. 'We are fighting with our lives in the *revolución*, first against *diez* and then *huerta*, and this *pendéjo* does not even know of Mexico City?!''

'Even I understand that without *revoluçion* there can never be peace. It is just that sometimes I forget things. I am an old man, you know.'

'Yes, I can see that,' he said, straining against rawhide straps, a sudden note of suspicion entering his voice. 'A very strange, old man, I see that now. Your body is so weathered and wrinkled it almost looks like a ...'

He stopped as a tall shadowy figure loomed between them. *El capitán del garra*, the nagual realised, recognising the beaked silhouette instantly.

'You were saying, *maestrito del escuela?*' *El capitán* demanded, sneeringly belittling the schoolmaster's professional status.

'Oh nothing, *capitán*,' the schoolmaster replied. 'He is just a *pendéjo* who does not even know there is a *revoluçion* in the country. I was just putting him right.'

'Are you sure you are not confiding where *you* hide the map?'

'If I had, he would not remember the next moment,' the schoolmaster chuckled, his chortles oddly juxtaposed against the background wails and curses.

'I am glad you find something amusing in all of this, *maestrito*. You will not be laughing when your turn comes, I assure you. And if I find you have lied, I promise you will void your *excramento* into your *pantalons* before I strangle you with your intestines.'

'Charming, isn't he?' my *compañero* said as *el capitán* swaggered away, continuing his round of the *camera de tortura*. 'Lucky he has no eyes to see what you are showing to all the world with your nakedness.'

'And what is that, my son?' the nagual said, already knowing the answer.

'The map, of course! Or do you take me for a *pendéjo*, too?'

'No! How could I when you are so learned and clever, with eyes to see what I, in my ignorance, cannot?'

'You mean you do not know?" The schoolmaster was incredulous.

'My son, you may not believe this, but I am only just born into this world. All I have seen of myself is a face reflected in the shiny brown boots of *el capitán*.'

'*En serio?*'

'Yes, my son,' the nagual sighed. 'But tell me, what do you see in this map on me?'

'A way to escape the town,' he grunted, 'If only I can loosen these thongs ...'

Sappatistas at work, undermining the dimensions, a sudden detonation below announcing that fact, the resulting explosion lifting a slab – and the nagual – high over the room. Making him think he had been transformed into a dirigible and was floating free of his moorings, as dreamily he regarded the broad beams of the floors above, collapsing like a house of cards, before he was deposited with a thump that knocked all the wind out of his sails, for the second time that day.

'Old man! Are you still alive?' a voice said from a long way above.

Stupid question, the nagual thought, resenting the schoolmaster's hands rattling his cage, brushing the dirt from his face. Didn't the clumsy oaf realise he was only tissue paper stretched over straw stays. 'Yes, my son,' the nagual managed at last, with an audible click as his dislocated jaw snapped back into place.

'I thought you were dead.'

'What happened?'

'Sappers, I suppose,' the schoolmaster said, grunting as he eased the nagual out from under a tarred wooden beam that had protected his body from the raining masonry.

'Now I remember,' the nagual winced, his ribs drawing black beads from the beam, as the schoolmaster hauled him out by the feet. 'The *sappatistas* below!'

'No, old man,' the schoolmaster grimaced, pausing to wipe the sweat from his smoke-blackened brow, 'You confusing "sappers" with the *zapatistas* in the south of the country, fighting under the leadership of *sub-commandante* Z.'

'This is true?'

'Yes, old man,' he answered tartly, ever the quintessential schoolmaster. 'Here in *el norté, las brigadás de la revolución* are commanded by one Doretero Arango, variously Pepe Gonzales and Francisco Villa, once a common bandit and now the talk of the country. You may even know him as Pancho.'

'Ah yes, *generalísimo* Pancho!' the nagual grinned, all his pains dissipating in an instant. 'Even I have heard of him! Though where or when, I cannot recall,' he said, regarding the schoolmaster with amusement as he crouched down beside him, rubbing his emaciated legs to get his circulation going. 'So the sappers below work for him too?'

'Yes,' the schoolmaster said distractedly, hands blurring as they worked away, 'Though how they tunnel through the mountains is quite beyond me, old man.'

'The tunnels already exist, my son!'

'They do?' the schoolmaster blurted, ceasing rubbing and looking up. 'Is that how you arrive? But I forget, you are the map, so how would you not know?

'The map is only what you see in me,' a nagual said, groaning with pain as the schoolmaster helped him to his feet. 'I know no more than you do, my son. Perhaps even less.'

'Stop right there! Move and I shoot to kill!'

No reward for guessing the owner of the voice, *el capitán*, stepping up with immaculately polished brown boots from concealment behind a ridge of rubble, aiming a long-barrelled Smith & Weston revolver with an unwavering hand.

'Oh no!' the schoolmaster groaned. 'How come you survived?'

'A charmed life, as you have already remarked,' *el capitán* grinned, his pressed khakis and fatigues reminding the nagual of a king cobra about to strike, as he advanced another few steps. 'I am protected by forces that you could not begin to grasp, even with your exalted intellect, *maestrito*.'

'Mere superstition!' the schoolmaster spat back. 'How the church and the state have pulled the *sombreros* over the eyes of the *campesenos* for centuries.'

'There are no *campesenos*!' *el capitán* declared, advancing a couple more steps. 'Just *locos* and leaders. And since you both fall into the first category, I am going to kill you.'

'And lose your only chance of finding the treasure?' the nagual interjected. 'Surely even you could not be that *loco, el Capitán?*'

'Who ... are you?' he demanded falteringly, as the nagual stepped out into a beam of sunlight shafting the stour of precipitated dust.

'I am the living map and gatekeeper of this reality, possessor of secrets undreamt of by your sceptical mind, *el capitán.* If I die, all this will cease to exist. Even you,' he said, feeling like the ancient of days, standing there pointing a withered finger. 'And the abomination you worship *en el castillo del* Chapultepec.'

Now he remembered the map anteceding all others: *la carta geographica* of his years. Started when? Before the Pleistocene era certainly, sprung into consciousness, precociously aware – in a mammalian sense – of the need to survive the predators of Eden, dinosaur parents blundering the garden, hazarding hatchlings just crawled out diaper swamps. The primeval Miocene era, when he was hot-housed on Homer and Herodotus, his father dallying with the idea of emulating Phillip of Macedonia's achievement in rearing a world conqueror, declaiming whole passages from memory verbatim – as Aristotle once recited over fair Alexander's crib – pushing a pram along summer lanes, pointing out Ithaca in the blue yonder, citing the example of Penelope's constancy – unlike some others he knew – fulminating on the dangers of Cyclops and Sirens, the lures of the lotus-eaters, his voice faltering as always when bespeaking his admiration for Xenophon's battle tactics. Subverting the young boy's unconsciousness to his purposes, peopling an unformed mind with long-dead superheroes, dedicating a pantheon to the ancient gods in his son's imagination, turning young thoughts towards conquest even before he was exiled from his attic room to boarding school at the age of seven, a *desperado* plotting escape and expeditions, all supplies of paper confiscated on account of his wilful disobedience, refusing to learn irregular Latin verbs, using the most readily available material to hand – his own hot-housed young skin, softest vellum, purest white as the first snowdrop in spring.

Dotted lines wrinkling antique parchment, still grist to his wrist after all these years, marking the way across slippery slates to the other attic skylight and the secret staircase below, not known even to the housekeeper. Peepholes strategically placed, eyes that peeled back on dusty ancestor portraits, the better to spy on his father come Saturday nights, when fraternal friends foregathered in a presbytery study – *los compañeros de la garra*, dressing up in black robes embroidered with ruby-clawed gold crosses. A right royal rookery of robbers, plotting coups wars and pestilence, unknowing there was a spy in the camp reporting on their activities to a higher command – the 'purple pimpernel', cloaked in invisibility, conferred by seven Talmudic seals tattooed to his breast in blue biro and, if the need for a quick exit interposed, seven league boots in felt-tip scribing on the soles of his feet, wings on his ankles allowing him to take whole mountain ranges in one bound or jump to Ursa Major to present his reports in person before the higher powers. All the stupendous events he had seen or would ever witness, his explorations through the snake-infested

Hindu Kush to a remote valley where he witnessed the extraordinary excavations of gold digging ants written about by Herodotus, the snowy mountain passes above commanded by abominable red-haired giants with back-to-front feet, or the time he humped it across the waterless wastes of the Makram on a camel. Every improbable adventure, painstakingly drawn in secret code on his body, *for eagle eyes only*. Indelible markings that were to outlast the nightly punishment scrubbings Helga administered in the tepid waters of the cast-iron bath, from which he would emerge, raw all over, only to be rubbed red, the tenderloin kid, smelling of rancid soap and mildewed towels, slinking off to hide by the only fire in the house, his wildly fluttering fledgling heart and steam giving him away, driven out the study by a bellicose bishop in flowing vestments and mitre, pursued with a venomously to the attic door and no-man's-land. His father brandishing the crozier of his office at the foot of the attic stairs, yelling, 'Get up to your room like a ruddy angel!' And, if he was in one of his 'black dog' moods, 'Get thee to Gehenna! Be gone this instant, accursed imp of Moloch!' Standing arms akimbo, eyes bulging dangerously, watching his young son crying his way up the stairs, while complaining to the housekeeper down in the kitchen in loud and anguished tones, demanding to know how the hell could he even begin to think of sermons and proselytising, when his repose was disturbed in this way.

His Father, and his father, standing behind him, a succession of elders in conclave, pivoted on plinths, lined up the hall whenever the young master glanced back, holding spirit lamps to shining stone faces ... faces he would ambidextrously doodle between fingers and thumbs, giving simulacrums mobility and the power of speech ... conversations to run over the horrible howlings of Cyclops, who every night crept out of the wardrobe outside his door, and the siren calls of banshees and worse, which, come hell or high water, slithered up from the black rocks at the foot of the stairs to lay siege to the portcullis door of 'Rufus the Wolf' – the reason he needed an escape route across the slates, and the map, in the first place.

Maps, sirens, quests; the Harijan housekeeper and her mother from the sugar-icicled north were in there too – Grandma and her tales of Woden and the Norns, subsumed by later stories from the classics, Greek heroes like Jason and his search for the golden fleece, the travails of Odysseus, Oedipus and the riddle of the Sphinx, setting down guide rails in the weirdness of a young master's mind.

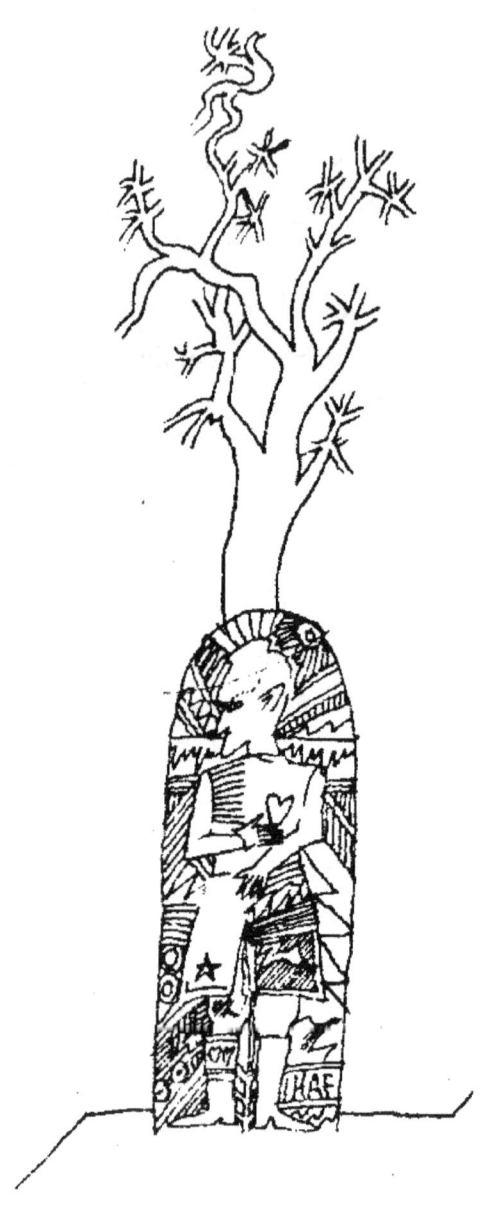

10. MAN DESTINED TO BE A TREE

For a vast stretch of subjective time, Double felt nothing, except for an absence of sensation, as if the darkness without had invaded his body and mind. What body and mind? So now he was a *phantom* double, needing confirmation he existed at all. OK, he thought, so he did have a mind, perhaps even an energy body too, for he did seem to intuit a cutaneous tickling where his toes should have been.

But proof he had, for, following another interval almost infinite in duration, he noticed the faint tickling was back and, more than that, well on the way to conquering the distant lands of phantom feet and ankles he sensed yet could not feel. Was it bind weed, he wondered, so tenaciously spiralling phantom lower legs, camping out on the strategic positions of phantom knees, surreptitiously advancing knees and thighs, reconnoitring the hidden dips and rises of phantom lumbar regions, sallying the secret valleys of his phantom groin where undergrowth was coarse and tangled on lower slopes of the bare uplands of his phantom stomach? Defining him, over a period extending for weeks and possibly months, from without if not within, a hollowed, inside-out double, occupying a void where skin and all the rest should have been.

Only the crepuscular creep of columns of tendrils on the march to remind him that he ever had shape and form. A body he once thought of as *his*, but now understood had all along been only property. Not his to do with as he liked, but chattel – the plaything of a god. Not the god of the Cristeros, AKA sweet Jesus Jaime, hamming it up on the cross. Nor Shem, the demiurge the Black Friars prayed to in their cathedral. But a power far more ancient. None other than the lord of this land, with a remit extending eight levels below. Yes, his feudal master, the arch-demon Lord Mictlán, who, by the terms of their contract, if he remembered right, still owed him a favour or two. There was even a certificate back at the hotel, setting out terms and conditions.

But his phantom mind was wandering. What use was such a contract, without pockets to put it in. What he would have given for pockets and the clothes that went with them. Jacket, shirt and trousers. How many pockets? Breast pocket, hip pockets, inside pockets, back pockets. A lot of pockets, ten at least on his usual ensemble, when he thought about it. What was it about pockets? Maybe it was something kept in one of his pockets, back when he had a body and clothes. Which pocket? Perhaps a hip pocket, on his left ... no, his right side. *Now* he remembered. That revolting gift of Helga's, the wrinkled dick of his forefather mummy. For regeneration, she'd said. Had she anticipated his present situation, he wondered, for, if so, she must have meant *his* regeneration, which was thoughtful. Some chance without a body. But perhaps he was wrong and he was presently in cryonic suspension, floating in a vat such as he remembered seeing in the mortuary vault under the cathedral after escaping all those talkative stiffs in the lowest level of Mictlán. As he recalled, the stone shelves were set out with vats, containing mummy parts bobbing in bubbling amniotic fluid. However those vats had clear glass sides, whereas he was now encased in something through which no light could pass. But hold on, he thought, realising that the darkness without, if not within, was not absolute.

Before his phantom eyes, two shady chinks floating on brimming ink, blacker than night. Glimmers, hardly enough to register, but the nonetheless – proving he did have eyes; by default a head and body; perhaps clothes too. Which took him back to the subject of pockets, and that mummy-dick in his left, no, he remembered, in his right pocket. If, indeed, the dick was as sacred and powerful as Helga had claimed, then it surely followed that if he visualised hard enough, perhaps it would materialise along with his clothes. And lo, there it was, just as he focused on the thought, its shape defined against his non-apparent hip by imaginary creeping vines. So at least he had trousers and was one dick up. Which, though hardly solving the problem posed by his absent body, did offer some hope. Was it possible that the baron had shafted him with a suppository, poisoned with the pineal gland of a Haitian black toad, as employed by voodoo high priests to turn the fresh dead, dug-up and spread-eagled, butt naked as when they were born, on the high altar of Baron Cimitère, permanently into living zombies?

Perhaps that explained how he had re-joined the congregation of the living dead? He even thought he sensed some previously noted tenebrous presences watching from the side-lines, dead but very much there, recumbent within their lead coffins on stone ledges recessed in the walls of that ecclesiastical court. Farcical though the trial had been, the crypt was impressive. Certainly as dark and foreboding as any court in the Old Bailey, he was sure. More foreboding, since this was the Shemite court. How was it he could recall the detailing of the stone impedimenta better now than during the proceedings? His trance state, he guessed. Then he had scarcely noticed that the groined vaults were delicately carved with a latticework of leaves and branches, spreading upwards from stout pillars resembling a stand of trees. Differentiated, one from another, by girth if not height, and cunningly wrought arboreal details of bark, branch, bolus, nook and cranny. The one behind the dais where the Shemite pope sat was massive, he recalled. What if he was immolated within and those two chinks floating before his phantom eyes were peepholes in its hollow stone trunk? Deduction, deduction, deduction. What was it Sherlock Holmes had said? Once you had eliminated the impossible, whatever remained had to be true, no matter how improbable. Well, something like that. Even in his deepening trance state his amnesiac memory defaulting. But at least he had established the salient facts.

None of which, however, went towards explaining the strange case of the advancing tendrils, now tickling his absence of ribs. At the conclusion of the trial – in his dream that was not a dream – delivering his verdict, the pope had directed that the prisoner was to be executed in the tree of death, which seemed just another way of describing crucifixion. Not the sentence he would have expected from the prelate of the Shemites. A religion, which, like Judaism, originated in the Middle East, where, until the Roman Empire extended there, stoning was the preferred method of execution. Perhaps crucifixion derived from Roman or Teutonic contact in the dark forests of northern Europe, where the tribes sacrificed their captives in trees? Slitting the throats of Roman legionaries, taken in raids further south, hanging them head down from upper branches. Draining their blood to feed the roots of Yggdrasil, the great tree that connected the nine enfolded worlds of Nordic belief. Sometimes in spring, if the captive was important enough, when morning mists curled about and the forest floor was wet with the dew of more than one world, his body would be bound in budding withes, leaving him to die from asphyxiation as greening withes slowly tightened, bundled into hollowed trunk of a standalone white oak such as were sometimes found in forest clearings, where lightning strikes were most frequent. The same trees that grew tall sheltered from the frequent lightning storms that struck the high *sierras*, safe in the shadowed depths of Happy Valley. Not like the blasted ancient white oak, standing at the forking of the path, on the bare lower slopes of three witchy peaks encountered during the long hike with Jaime.

Which brought to mind the black baron and what he knew of the lightning-struck family tree of the Hapsburgs – yes, yet more strange facts, made accessible only by a deepening trance state, first gleaned on long afternoons when it was raining on the lawns outside the windows of the presbytery study, and a lonely child had to content himself with pouring over the leather-bound books of a bishop's voluminous library – the British Royal family, themselves Hapsburgs, claimed descent from Woden. A wanderer from parts unknown, who, like another wandering sage of the middle Bronze Age, Confucius, had a penchant for dressing in black and communing with crows. Woden assumed the powers of a god after hanging head-down for nine days from the upper branches of a rowan tree, when he plucked out one eye and, casting it into a nearby cauldron as an offering, read the runes of life, the universe and everything with the other. Revealed in the spatter marks of his dripping blood congealing on red berries and brachiated leaves below that, with their usual thirteen divisions, symbolised time and were considered by the Teutons a charm against witches. Which was just as well, for the Norns, three mad sisters who lived at the base of the mightiest white oak of them all, were always skulking somewhere about.

Worshipped by the Teutonic tribes, who went on to conquer the Roman Empire, Woden gave birth to the saying about the one-eyed king in the land of the blind, and was known to successive generations as the man who measured the world. The same epithet accorded Voden, the red-haired giant wanderer from the east, who was welcomed as a living god and built Palenque before departing for mountains to the north. Where, according to one Mayan legend, his treasure was guarded by an ogress and her three identical daughters. Similarly, in the ancient European stories of the garden in the land where the sun went down, the three daughters of night, or the 'great ink' as he was referred to by the eponymous scribe of Samos in his famous scroll, guarded the golden apples of the sun. In Nordic legend, Woden is described wearing a long black cloak and wide-brimmed black hat.

Just as Voden is pictured in a Mayan codex. Was it then a coincidence that Malinché, the captive Aztec *bruja*, gifted by the Mayans to Cortez, persuaded the conquistadors to dress in black cloaks and matching hats *and* to delay their disembarkation to coincide with the date of the great god's return? A most special day, heralded for millennia in the Mayan long-count calendar, when the founding father would reclaim his Eden of Meso-America, lately held in trust by the Aztecs, who inherited the obligation from their predecessors, the Toltecs – a pyramid-building tribe with a liking for *mescal* ...

His penis promised physical regeneration to a phantom double, the last of the line of Inkethaton and, by default, the rightful claimant of the Inkethaton empire of the Americas, which once extended from Hudson Bay in the north to regions in the south where the Incas once ruled in his name. But only if with phantom teeth and jaws, he could masticate and then somehow ingest the horrible relic, after first removing it from his phantom pocket, which of course was impossible, not least because he was bound in the budding withes of a white oak tree from a sacred garden that, in the centuries following the conquest, had retreated the *sierras* to Happy Valley. Its wooded slopes finally reduced to cinders in the attack led by the mad Baron Hapsburg. The same who had interred him in this stone tree. Why? Because when it comes to pedigree, an Inkethaton always trumps a Hapsburg in the depth and reach of a family tree. The baron was just jealous of his roots, that was all. And besides, the bastard needed him out the way in order to pursue his bogus claim for the throne of Mexico.

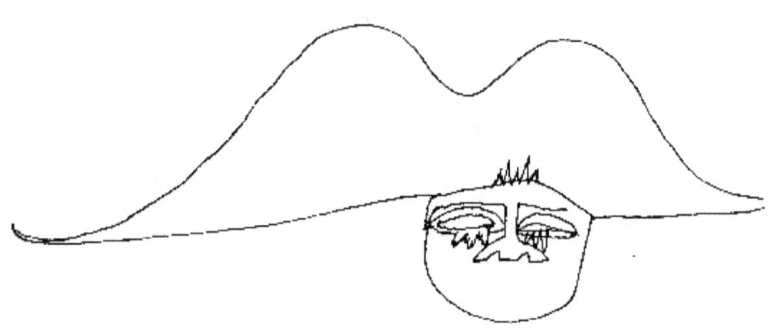

127

11.   LOST HIS BODY IN MEXICO

Movement behind two scratchy chinks cut out of pen and ink darkness, describing a pair of dolorous eyes. Peeking in at him, peeking out at a beam of moonlight, painting silver a threesome of sylvan nymphs entering a petrified forest glade in slow limbic glides from an offstage door. As, from beyond, a distant horn piped a slow lament that seemed to Double bound and stuffed in the hollow trunk of a stone tree, the opening bars of a funereal fugue marking his imminent demise. A dirge, beat by beat, step by step, in the worrying interweave of a dance, taking him down. Down to a time before, when he and his sisters played charades in the pillared attic of the old presbytery, that one Yuletide they were together, dressing up in theatrical costumes found in a wooden chest discovered among the possessions left behind by a disgraced bishop, lately departed for lands unknown. But that was then and this was now, Double reflected, reading cuneiform runes in the contrails of their hot breaths, hanging hoary in the still-chill air of the otherwise-deserted crypt. Ethereal eddies that, instead of dissipating, to his considerable surprise, only intensified in luminosity as three Norns circled closer, scuttling the carved roots of a stone trunk. The spectral trails of their coy advance, foxfire coursing arboreal pillars to pendentive vaults suspended above, silvering the impedimenta of stone leaf and branch, transforming a twilight crypt into the orchard of a garden that came back to him as if from a dream. A dream when he talked with his friend below dappled branches, boughed low by golden apples like the sun going down. Whereas the offerings above seemed more like crab apples, pale as the harvest moon, round as pearls and ready to drop. Like himself, he thought, dimly aware that, with every forward step, the damp chill of a threesome of silhouettes was further invading his bones. While, without a hollow stone trunk, spectral contrails snapped at three pairs of heels shuffling beyond, putting him in mind of a pack of weasels, jostling for space in the crepuscular half-light behind piercing eyes, glinting in the same butterfly winged masks his sisters always picked out when playing the game. The game when they were the Norns of Yggdrasil and he was the sacrifice – a captured Roman proconsul stripped of his toga, wearing nothing but a circlet of laurel leaves on the crown of his head, bound and tied to an attic pillar while owls hooted from rafters high above, waiting for their share of the spoils and bloody entrails when all was said and done.

Once again he remembered a pinking scissors attack in the dead of night, and his horror at his first sight of the bloody mess revealed below Amish covers, then, after the divorce, setting off on a coitus interruptus – finished before it started – journey. Getting it on, never getting it up, with strangers met in bars and dives who could never match him in desperation no matter how hard they tried. Doglegging it widdershins twice around the world, 'till at last he reached the town where the answers have no name. And now this, his sisters weaving their Norn spells around the base of a stone tree. A hornpipe fugue, taking him down ... down to that night in a hotel bed with three identical kitchen maids, and the question he now needed answering: how come they got it on when his rebuilt soldier never could with anyone else, his mother not excepted?

Cuneiform runes that was how, he realised, Lapland spells learned at Grandma's knees, whispered in his ears by an unholy threesome, conceived by a Catholic bishop and his harpy housekeeper when Saturn was ascendant and six planets were retrograde. Tricking him into believing he was at last successfully getting it up, *and* not only that, keeping it up all night – a performance even the *bruja* of the north, with all her evil wiles, hadn't managed to coax out of him – when in fact he was bound and tied to bed post. A *he* transformed into a *she*, shafted from behind by the stiff little dick of his forefather, while below a truncated root was sucked and blown. His sisters working as a team, taking turns to give him head, 'till he came so copiously they needed cups to collect the gummy stuff.

All this, spelled out in the cuneiform runes of contrary contrails hanging hoary in the chill air of the crypt, as the Norns wove one more spell. A rebuilt soldier-man at last budding into life and standing to attention as they danced around the swollen base of an old tree. This their parting gift in a relationship that, with the exception of two torturous episodes, had been one long goodbye. His final humiliation in a lifetime of humiliation and hurt that, by the regenerative power of a pharaoh's penis in his pocket, his little man should be made a working whole again, ironically just as he died, suffocated by evanescent green shoots coiled in a stranglehold around his neck.

All was quiet in the dark crypt, the sisters long gone, taking their foxfire with them. Yet, within a swollen stone trunk, where a bulging bolus was fuzzy with green sprouting shoots, something of Double persisted. Not so much a breath, but more than a last exhalation. A vaporous contrariness retaining enough of a fractured self to have thoughts. Yes, a true Inkethaten, persisting right to the very end, which duly unfolded when, engraven on the dark before him, appeared a face such as he remembered from before. The obsidian mask of a founding father, inlaid in a hollow within a stone trunk, incised with peepholes that now described the black eyes of Lord Mictlán.

'Father?'

'*Yes, my son.*' The voice was resonant and deep, not at all as a vaporous Double remembered, when, to an ear pressed against a breastplate, it was tinny and small.

'You have come?'

'*Yes, my son.*'

'But it's too late.'

'*Not too late to return a favour.*'

'But I'm dead.'

'*Yes, definitely, my son.*'

'So it's over.'

'*That is for me to judge.*'

'But how when my body is plant food?'

A vaporous Double in conversation with a mask in a crypt gestured to a tall trunk, fuzzy green with new growth from a bundled husk rooting in a stone hollow.

'*Immaculate plant food, as more than one family member is involved,*' Lord Mictlán chuckled.

'But how?' a vaporous Double insisted.

'*In Tláltipec, as elsewhere in Mictlán, there are always ways and means, besides which you still have memories to recover.*'

'What, more memories?' a vaporous Double said suspiciously.

'*Yes my son.*'

'What of particularly?'

'*It started with a book.*'

'What book?'

'*A forbidden book.*'

'Forbidden by whom?'

'*The last usurper to challenge my rule.*'

'Who exactly?'

'*Your predecessor on the fork behind you on the family branch of a great tree.*'

'I don't understand.'

'*How would you, when you are only a leaf?*'

'A leaf?'

'*The last leaf my son. Parched and blotched, but a true Inkethaton to the end, still holding on after the winter's gales.*'

'How come?'

'*Because you are the ghost who wouldn't give up!*'

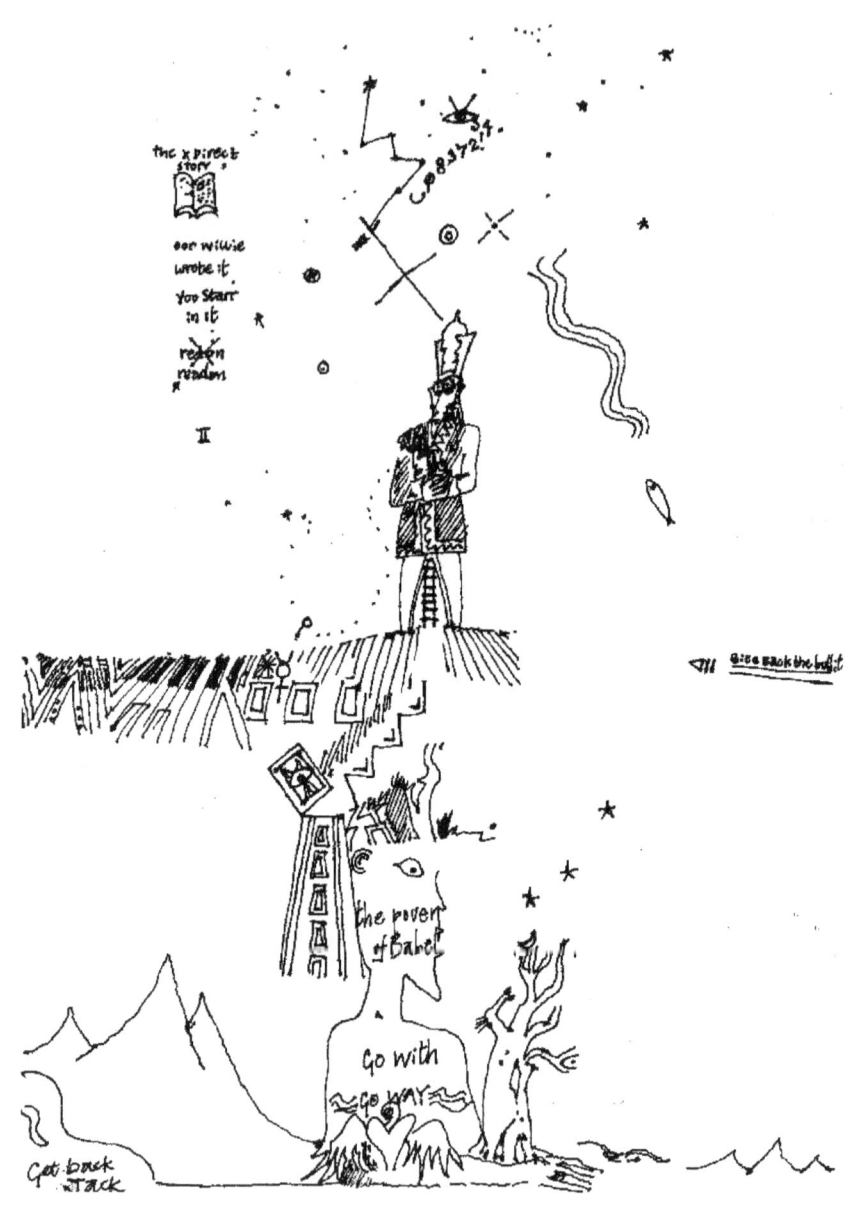

12.   THE X DIRECT-STORY

Revolutions take planning. But then comes the time for action, when all plans have to be chucked out the window. In Pancho's case – we are discussing the Mexican master bandit here – out the *railway* train window. But *ferrocarril* train window sounds so much better. *Ferro* meaning iron, forever associated in a young master's mind with Fiero, Villa's fearsome accomplice from the old days. Pictured in a forbidden book filched from a bishop's library, stepping down from his private freight car, branding a youthful imagination with his searing stare, standing second only to Pancho in a pantheon of revolutionary heroes. How a young boy wanted to be that man, stand next to the sun, the most loyal of Pancho's *generalísimos*, his doppelganger forever defending his back against sneak astral attacks – stars and bars, Yankee legions mostly.

Once, just to settle a barroom bet, Fiero gunned down a complete stranger across the street, merely to prove his point that men dying on their feet always fall forwards. Another revolutionary excess, also illustrated in the book, the killing of three hundred mercenaries; so called *colorados* in the employ of *crillo* cattle ranchers involved in a land grab of northern Mexico, some of their holdings bigger than mid-sized European states.

Fiero going about his business like a fox lose in a chicken coup, famously complaining to his adjutant, relaying reloaded pistols through the open shed door, that his trigger finger was tiring.

How such fierceness appealed to a young master, again and again returning to his favourite image of Fiero, wishing he could do the same to his elders, who, no matter how much they insisted, were not his betters. Starting with a bishop he now called *el capitán*. His disengaged father on battle manoeuvres again in his study below an attic bedroom. The old curmudgeon, pacing back and forth on creaking boards, rhythmically slapping his officer's swagger stick against his palm. A small boy's heart pounding in time with the sure knowledge that soon it would be his hide *el capitán* would be tanning. Time to pad out his pants with *The Picture Book of Mexican History*, those moustachioed heroes, his last defence against the tyranny of one patriarchs in particular.

But back to a slow train, incendiary of course, *el salamanda del sol* segmented as a worm, clanking across a blood red sky, trailing sparks to torch the tarbrush *mesas*. A string of fires under-lighting the haggard faces of ragged bands huddled atop the black hulks of freight cars. Divisions del Norté warming hands behind sandbagged gun emplacements, the revolutionaries sharing *mescal* and *muchachas*. Pretty girls with black hair tied up in red bandannas, swaying to revolutionary *carillos* played by revolutionary *mariachis*, while out front more *villaistas* rode the cow catcher, hanging over the rails on the look-out for mines left by the retreating federal army, sharing the cramped metal platform with a blanketed squaw clutching a baby to her breast and cooking *tortillas* over a flaming brazier.

'Where are you going?' came a shout from the darkness beyond. A peyote hunter, tall and lanky as a praying mantis crossed with bean pole, standing stock still, holding his white sombrero to his bare chest, arrested by that monstrous iron horse, snorting steam from a multitude of pipes and valves. Stopped before a busted section of track, where, under handheld flares, *villaistas* were laying out shining lengths of steel, levering pins and prising twisted rails from slatted sleepers.

'To the Town With No Name,' said the engine stoker, leaning on his shovel, presenting a coal-smudged face gashed by the whites of his eyes and teeth. 'Why don't you join us, *compadré?*'

'*En serio?*'

'*Cómo no?*' the stoker shrugged, 'When this civil war is your *fiesta* too!'

'You will then give me a poor peon with no place to call a home, a gun to kill the *gringo criollo* who has stolen the sacred lands of my Hutcholi ancestors?'

'*Sí!*' came a deeper voice, as a bulky man in a rumpled tweed suit, topped by a dusty bowler hat tipped at a jaunty angle, stepped out into the light of phosphorous flares. 'I, Pancho Villa, not a foking hidalgo son of a someone, as maybe you think, but the son of a *mulata* abandoned by a *barquinho* wineskin off the boat from Barcelona, who foking calls me "Doretero",[1] meaning my whole life I have to fight every *chingon* who insults my name, present you this pearl-handled pistol presented to me by General Scott of the US Army. And I promise you plenty bullets to kill the *Españolos* when we take that town. For four hundred years they have been stealing your treasure. The *oro* and the *plata*, that are the sweat of the sun and the tears of the moon for the long-suffering sons of Lord Mictlán.'

Revolutions require planning, and action too. But revolutions also need financing, certainly more pocket money certainly than a young master ever dreamed of. But money, in a land with a history of economic troubles such as Mexico, does not have the same intrinsic worth as elsewhere. Especially then, when the peso was in free-fall, foreign capital had taken flight and the federal government only controlled about a third of the country – and even less of the people.

---

[1] Was Doretero Arango (Villa) the inspiration for the Johnny Cash song 'A Boy Named Sue' – different names, same story.

All this was somewhat pedantically explained in *The Picture Book of Mexican History*. A footnote providing further information about the currency then in circulation – Austrian shillings, French francs and Mexican pesos from the days of Maximilian, dollars, deutchmarks and sterling to name but a few.

In this paper-chase of symbols and signatures, the problem was to determine which script had value and which had none. At least until Generalísimo Villa made his famous 'Counterfeit Decree', giving notice of an imminent change in banking practice. Presently, only bills personally signed by himself or one of his commanders would be accepted as legal tender. A deadline was set providing ample opportunity to exchange old and soon-to-be-defunct moneys for the new notarised bonds. Predictably, when the deadline duly passed, revolutionary coffers were overflowing with sheaves of hoarded dollars and other denominations so essential to purchase arms and munitions across the border.

By this means, the illiterate maestro of economic planning achieved what Marx and Engels had only dreamt of – if only within the six northern states controlled by the Divisions del Norte. Their beloved *generalísimo* at a stroke demolishing a reality construct imposed on successive generations, since King Croesus first coined it in Lydea. Yes, that fiction some people base their whole lives on, namely money. But even so *oro* and *plata*, those metals of the sun and moon, were as yet untarnished in the minds of the many celestial majesties retaining the power to promote new growth and breed worms in the hardened hearts of the criminal master classes.

There was one place where any amount of gold and silver counted for less than a mine of beans. The Town With No Name, under siege these past months by an advance contingent of *villaistas*. All supplies having long since run out, its defenders reduced to a diet of the scorpions then plaguing the town. Even each other, after cannibalism became a privilege of rank, by edict of *el capitán* of the black crow brigade. With his clipped moustache, permanent scowl and fixed stare, bearing an uncanny resemblance to the master of the presbytery and as mean a *hombre* as you could ever wish to meet. Transplanted by the dreams of a young master to the cauldron of revolution, defending the federal government treasury, the *Castillo de la Dinero*, its vaults stacked to bursting with ingots of useless *oro* and *plata*

El capitán of the claw was fascinated with all things yellow, pus, bile, snot, diarrhoea, especially when it turned liquid and dribbled the inside of his legs, scaly with worm casts, as happened every full moon when the *gusano de diablo* sheds its skin. *El capitán* never missing the opportunity to commune with the golden-clawed monster transmitting electrical impulses to his brain. In the privacy of his personal latrine, on his knees, stirring body wastes in porcelain pan with a swagger stick. Before belting up his pressed khaki trousers and stepping out into the sun – the only yellow he didn't much like, since it burnt his sensitive skin.

Gold was another yellow he liked. Oh yes, he liked that very much, especially in 'bricks', the way the guards in the *Castillo de la Dinero*'s basements called ingots. Now *that* was something to build a house with. Sometimes sitting alone in his vaulted latrine, he would imagine his dream *castillo*. A gold edifice, of perhaps ten thousand bricks, topped by twenty-four carat towers that would never tarnish nor require any maintenance or cleaning, as they were made out of the precious metal. The rooms inside, much the same, no decoration, just gold bricks, course on course, of course.

Yellow hair on busty bitches jackbooted up to lardy thighs, he also liked, especially the thatch he was forced to look up to. Well, perhaps that wasn't quite accurate, he was uncontrollably attracted to blondes, the bigger and more bossy the better, but their hair had to be the exact right straw shade, too light or dark a tone and his feelings turned to revulsion. Once he had found himself on a flea infested mattress in a brothel in the port of Veracruz with a most gorgeous jackbooted *fräulien* with the biggest boobs ever, just off a banana boat from

Hamburg, but then, he just as he was about to press home his golden rod, he had noticed her flax was black at the roots.

Before leaving the establishment he was obliged to pay a hefty surcharge for the stripes the whore would bear for the rest of her days. A beating well worth the pesos and one he often thought about with pleasure afterwards.

The yellow he loved and, but for a golden-clawed worm pulling on his gut-strings, would have reigned supreme in his firmament, was the *amarillo* of the auricula primrose. His first sighting each time *primavera* came around never failing to induce a profound, if temporary, change of mood. A memory of how life could have been and yet might be, if only the *sierras* of the world would bloom primrose.

Scryed in wavering shadows on the sloping walls of an attic bedroom, the Grim Reaper scuttling desert sands. Or perhaps that scythe was really a claw dripping with venom? Hard to make out, those shadows doubling on deeper shadows. *Los cardinales*, a coven in conclave? A rookery of hooded crows crowded on a *caldera*? Centre circle, *las tres hermanas*, no doubt about the identity of those three *brujas* stirring up seismic change in magma-mantled depths.

Slips of yew, tongue of *chihuaha*, liver of kabbalistic

Jew, *gringo*'s nose, *tzitzimime* wing, *mescal* worm's sting ... yes, all that and more into a *caldera* went, while, far below, *el salamanda del sol* clanked ever-closer across desert plains.

Over the years Fiero had served Villa well. Husband and spouse were never as close, except perhaps in the original meaning of wife, the distaff mate who weaves the bed sheet. Bedfellows then? No. But accomplices, yes. Drawn together by the weird of their lives, the weft and woof holding together a great tapestry that was to set the design of the century. All the revolutions that followed patterned on theirs. Lenin and Trotsky, taking their cue from the Mexican triumvirate, Villa, Fiero and Zapata. As they in turn had been inspired by Prince Falling Eagle, executed after he refused to reveal the whereabouts of the Aztec treasure smuggled out of Tenochtitlán. And Cuauhtémoc's heroes? Surely, included among them, Votan, raised by the Tzendal tribe to the status of a god – the man who measured the world and gave meaning where before there was none. Indivisible with Wotan, master of the wode and primogenitor of revolution, who unchained the 'fury' and brought down the Roman Empire – Spartacus, Wallace, El Cid, Robespierre, Toussaint, Washington, Garibaldi, Paine, Muir and countless unnamed heroes ... even a young master ... his avatars.

Stepping down from his box car, dripping warm blood onto cold rails below, Fiero scooped a handful of dirt and stood up, watching as a gust of warm wind scattered the sand slipping his blood-stained fingers towards the emerald light glittering on the distant ring-stone *cordilleras*, heralding dawn over the eastern horizon. It was the time he called the hour of the dog, neither day nor night, when his mind was sharpest and only coyotes were about. A fine time for contemplating those three northern-facing peaks, hiding from the world the town where he had been born. The snow-capped summits of three little sisters, darkening as massive thunder heads reared from the south.

'Even the mountain gods are with us!' a nearby voice declared as, simultaneously, a distant clap of thunder rent the thin sierra air.

Fiero recognised that rich baritone. Just as well, for he had shot men for creeping up on him unawares. Interrupting those precious private moments, usually before the dawn, when he cast out the demons perpetually hitching rides on his shirt tails. Demons he saw skulking in long shadows at the end of day, lurking in the eyes of friends and strangers. Most especially in ejaculations his victims often voided, spurting their souls at the moment of death. Sperm stains he studied, just as Woden did aeons before. Killing was a dangerous business, and the worst of it was the voices others rationalised as conscience but Fiero knew were just ghosts with which the world was thickly populated. Legions he would one day join, but before that he meant to have himself a time adding to their numbers, something he thought of as pre-posthumous revenge for the horrible threat of life eternal promised by the priests who raised him in the Town With No Name.

'Pancho!' Fiero said, without turning round, a grin splitting his tombstone face as it always did when he spoke that name – the *cabrón* was a living legend, even if he was an asshole who would not take a drink. Despite that, there was still more fun in him than a *cantina* of *locos* with firecrackers exploding in their *pantalonés*.

'You are through talking to *puta gringos?*' Fiero demanded. 'At last we can get to the action?'

'Already the telegraph wires are singing, Fiero,' Villa said softly. 'Today their newspapers will be full of our victory in Zacatecas. The *gringos* like winners, not losers. Huh?'

'That side I leave to you, Pancho,' Fiero grinned fiercely, his love for his *companero* a black bird clawing at his breast. 'I am thinking of what I just learn from a federal army *padre* before he dies.'

Pausing, Fiero reached for his pack of *cigarillos and* lit a lucifer with a practised flick of a thumbnail, cupping hands, shielding the match from the dry Sonora wind, drawing deep on smoke while Pancho waited patiently, standing with hands clasped behind his long back, looking across the desert at the emerald light of dawn, spreading on the eastern horizon.

'There is a second tunnel into the town. Up to now only known only to the priests of the worm,' Fiero said, hoicking a great gob of spit just as a yellow-hooked scorpion scuttled across the sand by his boots, drowning the insect in a phlegm of a far deadlier predator, reminding the young master scrying the scene in wavering shadows on a bedroom wall that, in the armoury of arachnids and storytellers, hooks invariably count as claws, whereas the claw, in essence, is a multitude of things, pain mostly, but the torment of pleasure too.

13.   PANCHITO

It takes claws to get a grip on reality – any reality – and in the casino of the cosmos, realities come in packs and are constantly shuffling. That's where blind hope comes in. The hope that springs eternal. The steady hope of young minds, dreaming a way out of penal regimes imposed by beastly parents. Like this tunnel undermining the defences of the Town With No Name in one direction and, in the other, signposting the fortress of a foreign god that, to Pancho Villa, was ultimate enemy, since on that rock lived the procurer of the suffering of his people over centuries. Presented with that choice, what other course did he have but to turn towards that citadel,[2] taking with him Rudolfo Fiero and the Divisions del Norté, leaving only a squad of

---

[2] In the annals of warfare perhaps the most daring unrecorded chapter was Pancho Villa's underground assault on the Vatican, culminating in the capture of a sacred gourd stolen from his people. Pancho finally died in 1922, his last words: 'Tell them I said something clever.' Three years after he was buried, his body was dug up and his skull removed to a private ossuary in Norfolk, Virginia, which houses a vast collection of stolen bones of people who, over the ages, earned the enmity of an ancient secret society, which numbers many US presidents, living and dead, among its members. Pancho Villa's skull is displayed in a case on a shelf alongside the skulls of Cromwell, Thomas Paine, Eva Peron, Geronimo and Charlie Chaplain to name but a few.

sappatistas under the command of the young master Panchito, who, with his ferocity in combat, tantrums and transformations, more than made up for what he lacked in stature and experience. A pint-pot *generalísimo* in overlarge *pantalons*, it was true, but one for whom he had high hopes.

Over the centuries the tunnel had served the priests well, its worn passages worm-smoothed and beaten by the traffic of countless sandaled feet. Papal nuncios among the delegations passing unseen in and out of the Town With No Name, spiriting away native treasures to gather dust in the vaults of the Vatican. Heretical manuscripts, such as the famous Codex of Uxmal, which included a catalogue of secret names of god known only to the Tzendals, supposedly burnt in the sixteenth century by Bishop Landa. Relics like the sacred Gourd of Coatlicue, containing the sacred seed of Quetzalcoatl, which must be rattled at the end of every epoch of the sun, to summon the new world.

A new world Panchito longed for, this worm passage tunnelled under ditch-dull realities, where rules were undeviating as rails set on beds of stone, to a door fixed by blind hope in the sacristy of a cathedral that was perhaps the best least-known wonder of Christendom. Its towers and transepts, flying buttresses, fluted vaults of the thousand polished porphyry pillars purloined from the temple of Amun-Ra on the banks of the Nile; the vast echoing basilica, its pilasters, pediments and niches crowded by gargoyles and gilded statuary; the rock crystal rose transept window representing untold generations of indentured native labour, every pane painstakingly ground by hand; the interior of the great dome painted with an enormous trompe l'oeil picturing Shem descending in a blaze of glory to rescue his 'chosen' people; while the exterior of the dome was sheathed in Aztec gold, smelted, it was whispered, from the great disc of the sun and the girdle of Coatlicue, plundered from the temples of Tenochitlán – all of it shaped out of the magma of creation by a questing young mind ...

Questing. That was the ticket, but where? Into the dark continent located between his none-too-clean ears ... largely unexplored, with only a few scattered settlements at the confluences of turgid rivers and strategic high places, such as the Town With No Name. Nameless because ... because names were power, marking the awesome finality of things. The world might end if he let slip that secret. Better to forget, buffeted as he was by so many strictures from without ... contradictory admonitions from father and housekeeper, acting like leaden clouds, piling up to obscure the sun, causing thunderstorms, hail and dyslexia ... double-double trouble in later years, when exiled from home and hearth, let down by all but a few of those he had counted as friends, he wandered far and wide, confused by countless correspondences internal and external, searching for himself in a looking-glass world. All of it shaped out of the magma of creation by an amnesiac god, gone walkabout these past billion years, searching for his maker beyond the stars, Chronos, the father of time, who ate his children, as good a name as any other for the bungling architect of creation, imposing strictures, where there had been none before ... prescriptions and admonitions ... rules made to be broken by those who followed. Questers and jokers, shuffled out of the pack, cast aside by the cosmic croupier, going their own way, shaping reality out of torments imposed by others, the unknown soldiers of the future, living unrecognised by their fellows. Moving the dead weights of the masses with the power of their dreams.

The captain (mentioned twice in dispatches) was not amused, to put it mildly. Pipsqueaks, like that demon spawn of his loins, should be seen and not heard, obey orders without question and, like good little mice, should only squeak when squoken to. He wasn't a monster, as his son seemed to believe, nor was he a philandering bishop, as the young master had once accused him, nor a kabbalist in league with the nine lords of Xibalba (wherever that was), plotting coups and pestilence, destabilising perfectly legitimate regimes the world over, a notion so completely irrational it spoke volumes for the state of the boy's mind, either that or it had been implanted by his mother, a woman much subject to delusional fancies, who once claimed she was a sword swallower run away from the circus and would keep insisting her wedding vows only obligated her to keep the former presbytery clean, serve three hot meals a day (never once in all the years served on time), in return for the housekeeping expenses – and certainly not conjugal rights.

Not that the captain was too bothered in that regard, the fires of passion having cooled to an arctic frigidity since that fateful first meeting when, taking a shortcut over the moors after West Wickham Cross, he had stumbled upon her bathed in golden sunshine, spreadeagled in the heather, performing her devotional rituals to Helios, as she explained later, putting him in a compromising position, from which he sometimes doubted if he would ever recover.

The hastily arranged marriage, another of her mad notions, a midnight wedding in a deconsecrated church operating as a furniture repository, the ceremony performed by a part-time pastor, apparently some Lapland relation from north of the Arctic Circle, an imbecile reindeer herder hardly able to recite the matrimonial vows, bringing a curtain down on his bachelorhood. That perfect state every man is born to, and every man despises until it is too late. Alas, he had fallen prey to the most immoral and unscrupulous women it had been his misfortune to meet.

That first meeting so precisely matching his masturbatory fantasies of amatory assignations with amazons in lofty public places, he sometimes suspected she was a harpy sent by the Norns to punish him for wasted seed. A suspicion that would lead one to suspect the retired captain was a wanker and of a paranoiac turn of mind, as indeed he was, a tendency induced by the strange events that that regularly befell him. Happenings invariably anticipated in dreams, both nocturnal and waking, and all the more puzzling for that reason. An idle fancy, a name or a face would take root in his mind and, before too long, something akin or approximating would take place, leading him to suspect either that time followed a circular direction and was forever coiling back on itself, crossing and re-crossing arbitrary but nodal points - worm singularities, as some modern scientists called them - or that there was some supernatural agency at work.

His Helga, despite her harpy origins, was just a fact of life he had to get along with. But relations with his son were a different matter. Badly brought up and boorish as the lad was, knowing only the headlong charge, all was not lost yet. Perhaps the best thing would be to remove the boy from his mother's malign influence. A regime of boarding school and summer camps, and hang the expense. A course suggested by his confidant Mr Crook, as good a friend as a man could hope to have. The lawyer never interrupting a captain's interminable discourses, which always had the same end in view, the erection of a monument of might and majesty, casting a suitably long and eclipsing shadow. Testifying for all time one mortal's life and achievements. That last entry a blank space in his scheme of things for, though he had always known he was destined for greatness, indeed that the Norns themselves had decreed it should be so, chanting over their fabled cauldron that doubled as a whirlpool, never seen until it was too late by sailing ships plying the icy waters in search of the Isles of the Blessed at the very limits of the world, he could never quite decode that pre-determining primordial sentence. Even though there still resounded within the *wyrd* that was the warp and woof of him, Clotho, the blind sister, singing as she span, announced a life of worth and grace that would raise a star in the firmament to light the footsteps of those that followed. Yes, something like that, he was sure. But what the star? Where the constellation? His firmament had been obscured by clouds rolling up from the west ever since he'd taken that shortcut across the heath and over Wickham Moor. Unbeknownst crossing into one of those nodal singularities when time worms back on itself. Too preoccupied to see the danger presaged by dreams and omens over the years, until it was too late. Yes, he could not blame himself for falling, knowing as he did, no man of mettle could have withstood her siren lure. Her ample charms, acting upon him as the sticky secretions of a Venus fly trap, as drawn into that clawed embrace, he fell, his futile struggles, only ensnaring him further. His bachelor idyll fast fading to an arcadia in memory, golden days when winged thoughts were as clear and far ranging as the beam of the Pharos Lighthouse, seventh Wonder of the World, calling to ships over stormy seas, warning of submerged reefs, the Fata Morgana and sundry other dangers, lighting triremes and barques to harbour and safety, bearing exotic cargo from every quarter of the known world, and some from beyond, fabulous feathers of birds of paradise from the garden of the west, 'Quecha' cocaine for the sons of pharaohs and their courtesans, silk and sandalwood from Cathay, unicorn horns and giant ostrich eggs from the court of Prester John, the despotic but benevolent Christian emperor of sub-Saharan Africa, where men were blue and grew nine foot tall, possessed two heads and lived more than five hundred years.

All this recorded in the scrolls and manuscripts of the Alexandria Library, like that city's lighthouse, the greatest in the world, containing the totality of knowledge then known to man, most of its four hundred thousand volumes consumed by the great fire in AD 391 bringing the curtain down on the Heroic Age, ushering in the Dark Age that was to last a thousand years, when all Europe, with the exception of its western fringes, reverted to savagery and men became as brutish as swine. All this predicted by Erasmus of Phillipa, patriarchal philosopher, kabbalist and cosmologist, founder of Alexandria Alternative School of Anatomy, and propounder of the 'Grand Central Theory,' also known as the 'Junction Box Theory'. The first attempt to explain nature of the world and everything, rubbished by his great contemporary Aristophanes – who also dismissed the writings of Anaxarchus[3] – and later rejected by Copernicus, but, despite this, in the opinion of a captain, was a profound contribution to the sum of all that is known, even though there was no monument nor mausoleum dedicated to his name.

A matter the captain meant to put to rights, just as soon as he published his magnus opus, intriguingly entitled *The Book of Tell Tale Signs and Other Portents* and, including among the essays, treaties on Erasmus' great works lost in that calamitous fire, reconstructed by

---

[3]When Alexander learned from Anaxarchus of the infinite number of worlds, he wept, but then he laughed with joy when Anaxarchus told him of the openings into these worlds, and how he might seek them. Asked by Anaxarchus what prize could justify so perilous a journey, Alexander replied, 'That for which I sacked the cities of Asia, and searched near enough a world, the *treasure with no name.*'

proven kabbalistic method from the sole surviving text, a charred papyrus, inherited from his unknown mother, according to the Coptic nuns who first raised him, a blonde giantess run away from the harem of the last Caliph of Cairo, who was known to favour big women.

How big is big? Big is big, it goes without saying. But big is bigger than small, and small is bigger than wee. Using a well-tried kabbalistic formula, 4.5 counts as 1.25 when comparing big titties to big willies. Unfortunately, given his predilection for oversized broads the captain was not over endowed in that department, at least in his own estimation, downsizing his own while over estimating his rivals', usually glimpsed in stolen sideways glances and always in underground urinals. One penis in particular – a close encounter in the Bakerloo Station toilets on the Piccadilly Line, wartime London – providing the inspiration for his damascene conversion, when scales fell from his eyes, as belatedly he realised even a weenie cannon can fire a mighty shot, and the phallic symbolism of Erasmus' speculations on the origins of the universe at last became clear.

As it says in the good book, knock and you will be answered – well, eventually. But what if nothing happens? Kick heartily, and again if needs must. But what if there is still no answer, and that door has been reinforced by gold plates inches thick, as was recently ordered by *el capitán*, barred, bolted and barricaded from without? When all else fails, and authority in its citadels, in this case a cathedral, proves deaf to the clamour below, take the revolutionary option, blow away that door and some of the foundations too, as happened after the young *generalísimo* directed his *sappatistas* to lay charges, pressing the plunger himself, fulfilling an ambition nursed since nursery years, ever since he first learnt about dynamite and its creative potential for change.

KA-BOOOOM!! Surely they used kryptonite, thought the young *generalíisimo*, for the blast seemed out of all proportion to the tiny amount of sticky stuff impressed into hinges and locks.

KA-BOOOM-BOOOOM!! Roll that one again, considered the pint-pot *generalíisimo*, as came a series of answering echoes from lower depths, the blast reverberating cavernous walls below the catacombs, where hunter's bones lay strewn with the skeletal remains, sabre-toothed tigers, long-toed lemurs, ground sloths, giant hominids, hairy mammoths, long-horned bison, even a few creatures of legend, basilisks, chimeras, among the predators and prey, entombed a hundred thousand years, ever since the violent cataclysm that ended the world known as '4 Sun' by the Maya, fire descending from the sky, as a comet crashed into the earth.

KA-BOOM-BOOM-BOOM!! Now there were counter echoes, even louder, from above, peeling detonations that sounded exactly like rolling thunder, which of course they were. The thunder storm arrived right on cue, blanking out the explosions, even to the Brethren of the Worm, celebrating vespers in the basilica a few levels above. The subject of the evening sermon, a brief summation of the events that led to the great schism with the mother church in 1859, coinciding with the publication of the *Origin of the Species by Natural Selection* by the false prophet Charles Darwin (also the author of the lesser-known *Vegetable Mould and Earthworms*). Father O'Flaherty giving the lowdown on the dramatic discovery of the fossilised hulk of a boat in an icy cave near the summit of the highest of three little sisters, which could only have been Noah's Ark. Ten emerald tablets found inside, giving the ultimate truth that this world is a lie, all walking, crawling, grunting, talking, living forms, with the exception of the progeny of the one worm, were but incubuses dreamed up by a childish god, petulant in his tantrums and transformations, given to destroying his creations in fits of pique, using any ready means; piss, vomit, fire and asteroid impact. This revelation causing the brethren to reinterpret holy writ and discard all but one of the books of the Bible after the story of Noah, that exception being the Epistle of John, since it dwelt on the wickedness of man, retribution and coming calamity when the world of '5 Sun' would finally end by wormquake, as the golden-clawed denizen of the deeps roused from slumber at last.

Although all but one of Erasmus' works perished by fire – and even that of doubtful provenance, since the papyrus in the captain's possession had never been authenticated by any accredited expert in the field – the pedant is not a complete cipher. Aristophanes described him as a big man with an ugly red nose, covered in bumps and gristle, which was his most readily recognisable feature, 'marking him out from other mortals, as a cracked pot stands out on the potter's shelves'.

Simeon of Tarsus, with whom Erasmus was personally acquainted, said he was 'much given to making jokes' and was an excellent storyteller, though his stories generally erred on the 'fantastical side, dwelling as they did on the junctures and dislocations between the worlds of gods, men, and lesser creatures'.

Another source, the blind poet Hecatitus the Simple, insisted he was a 'down to earth salt of serious aspect, who invariably rose a'fore the cock crow, and was always diligently occupied in one study or other'.

What all the commentators did agree on, however, was that Erasmus disappeared during a lightning storm in the Sinai Desert in 63 BC.

According to one apocryphal account, 'the wrath of Amon descended upon the braggart in a great whirling fog. And when the black cloud finally lifted? Erasmus of Phillipae was no more to be seen'.

A singular occurrence that has passed into history without much examination.

'Poor old Erasmus of Phillipa passed away.'

'Oh yes? And how did he go?'

'In a thunder storm. A black whirling cloud descended and bore him away!'

'You don't say! Happens all the time to these new philosophers, an occupational hazard, I suppose. But what do you expect when you go round impugning the gods as he did. Why only last week in the market I heard him ...'

Just so. Always plenty scoffers about with ready opinions, yes, too many around in old Alexandria to include here. What mattered to the captain was the manner of his hero's death. Uninformed historians, passing over the remarkable occurrence with scarce a backwards glance, unknowing or unmindful of Erasmus' words on the subject, as quoted by Hecatitus the Simple: 'Since death is the apogee of life, the moment is a study in itself. Great warriors seek glorious death in battle, miserable misers seek miserable ends, while seekers groping for answers all their lives, find truth at last.'

Trawling back from that moment, decoding the 'Alexandria Papyrus', the captain found it appropriate that Erasmus had been uplifted to heaven on a tornado, since so many of his speculations had concerned the forces set into motion by whirling twisting things, the 'wormholes' that were the windows and doorways into unseen worlds, 'through which gods and demons flitted at will'.

Time, Erasmus maintained, was a collective conspiracy; a story driven mass fabrication, born of blinkered lives, and a need to delude ourselves into believing events proceed in a sequential pattern. Life is chaos, and any sense of continuity a complete illusion. Reality, as he explained it, was a spherical envelope existing in a void, perhaps populated by countless such envelopes, maintained by the thoughts of the resident sentient creatures – certain individuals, whether by intention or unconscious attribute, in dreams or waking, possessing the ability to rupture the skein holding back the void, causing a temporary or even terminal collapse of that reality, as happens at the end of every 'age'.

The foregoing being the cause of many otherwise unexplained events, such as the sense of knowing a place before one has visited it, or foretelling the day and manner of one's death, as Erasmus did. Predicting the day a wormhole would spirit him back to a far country, where friends were waiting. This distant land none other than the fabled garden of the golden apples,[4] sought by questers and *sappatistas* alike, seeking escape from ditch-dull replicant realities, each simulacrum a paler copy than the last, the wish fulfilment of bureaucrats and legislators dreaming of open-prison societies staffed by sadists, graveyard worlds where hope lay long buried, patrolled by police and *padres*, where rules ruled, disorder reigned and crime paid only those in the know.

Those in the know, including the captain, transposed to a revolutionary reality that was anything but dull, at the behest of his worm master ... his son and heir, though *el capitán* would hardly have recognised him, disguised as the lad was in thigh-high buckskin boots, improbably droopy moustaches under an overlarge *sombrero*, putting his best foot forwards, determined to roust occupying vermin from the Town With No Name ...

This was *his* reality and he wouldn't share it. Never mind those armed guards, sheltering from torrential hailstones, crack federal troops huddled over in the entrances to those mines or that the hook-nosed *capitán*,

---

[4] In most accounts the garden is guarded by a giant worm or dragon, this perhaps a clue as to the means of getting there.

mumbling under his breath, looking out from under a striped awning, anxiously checking for signs the thunderstorm was abating, was his father. No, that was a louse, parking his behind where he wasn't welcome, touring the plaza in his palanquin in the style of an Indian raj, supported on the stout shoulders of four brawny soldiers, circling a great erection rising wraithlike above the Town With No name, its upper reaches lost in plumes of mist ...

What was *el capitán* so rabidly mumbling?

'Money. Money. Money. Money. Money. Money. Heheh. Money. Money. Money. Money. Money. Heheh. Money. Money. Money. Money. Money. Heheh. Money. Money. Money. Money. Money. Heheh. Money. Money. Money. Heheh. Money. Money. Money. Heheh. Money. Money. Money. Heheh. Money. Money. Money. Money. Money. Money. Money. Heheh. Money. Money. Money. Money. Heheh. Money. Money. Money. Money. Money. Heheh. Money. Money. Money. Heheh. Money Heheh. Money'

The word is so real, so central to so many realities, so rooted in shit, it did not distort or lose its meaning, despite the occasional snigger, even after the foregoing repetitions. Most words begin to defray after three or four, while some words, carry little if any meaning – at least in this bubble reality – like god, for instance ...

God. God. God. God. God. God. God. Cod.[5] God.

The word just refuses to stand up and bark, unlike its reverse, the word 'dog', which is ready to wag a tail with just one saying.

God, give me some money! A prayer that never works. One has to apply a different appellation if one wants the sky to shit gold. Such as, 'Panchito, give me some money!' The pint-pot *generalísimo* on the case, with his personally notarised revolutionary bills illustrated by his smiling countenance on one side, and on the other a hand drawn map giving the location of a crock of gold, at the ready. Just in case *el capitán*, with his machinations succeeded in rupturing the envelope, and punching through to the void, bringing an end to all this. The last chapter ... the last page ... and all because one word was done to death. A word no amount of repetitions could unstitch. A word that moved men's lips, more than any other, whether waking, in sleep or in prayer. That word was money, defraying because of the extraordinary conditions prevalent in that Mexican reality, the cumulative effects of hyper-inflation and so many devaluations, the collapse of the banking system, the bandit insurgency, the corruption, the worm ...

---

5. The Noviet, an Eskimo people, living on the island of Novia Sibir in the Laptev Sea, believe they are descended from the great cod who lived in the Primordial Sea and that the first men had tails and swam in a reef dotted with luminous starfish, which is the Milky Way, still lighting the sky at night.

Money might have lost much of its value, but *oro*, that metal so beloved of Croesus, and all the worm masters that followed, still reigned supreme in the firmament; as long as it did, the grand central reality through which all wormholes were routed would hold. But remove that pillar – that mighty trunk of Yggdrasil, the world tree – and reality collapses, or so reasoned *el capitán*. He was no worm master, with the forces of the multiverse at his command. The appellation of common jobbing torturer will do, he thought, looking up at the Babel of wooden scaffolding, pit props plundered from below, causing the collapse of mines and catacombs as far afield as Rome itself, every tree from a hundred miles around, supporting the great bronze barrel aligned on the sun. A thousand feet high already and, with each casing added, mounting ever higher.

Like a salamander, segmented of course, *el capitán* thought, wiping away a tear, temporarily blinded, as at last the sun emerged from silver-scrolled cumulus that promised an end to the storm. Just as well, for that was the moment Panchito chose to descend from the cathedral, taking the steps three at a time, running towards concealment behind the great pile of ingots, stacked high as a house ramparted with battlements and towers. Golden bullets, piled in the shadow of the great barrel, ready to fire at the sun, when *el capitán* judged the moment was right.

That moment was fast approaching. High noon, thirteen o'clock by local time. Denouement for the reality maintained since the conquest by the thoughts of its indigenous population, the vast majority living in fear and trepidation, the value of the pesos in their pockets shrinking in proportion to the rising paranoia, terrified as to what might come next, the approaching Shemite millennium, brought on by the prophesies of a local, supposedly native, seer, *el espiritu,* who no one knew, but everyone knew of – actually *el capitán*'s mouthpiece, Father O' Flaharty.

Mr Crook by another name, disseminating rumours through the confessional, sometimes disguised as a *borracho* in the local cantinas, telling of the approaching end, when six thousand years after creation, the sun of the fifth millennium would crash to earth and worms would breed in the gathering darkness, eating everything from within, multiplying exponentially until at last there was nothing left to eat and they consumed themselves. The new world[6] that followed, sterile and dead as the moon itself, where nothing moved except long shadows, tracking over a vast desolation caused by the greed of man.

---

[6]New world order: see any US dollar bill for details, under Nuit's eye in the pyramidion.

It was done. Even as the derrickmen up on the scaffolding slotted the last bolts into place, a squadron of troops stepped back from the breech, more than a thousand feet below. Saluting smartly at *el capitán*, looking on from the palanquin, signalling that their job was complete, the house of gold successfully dismantled and ten thousand bricks tamped down in the barrel, bedded on a kiloton of explosives, and the fuse at last laid.

A long blue twist of paper extending perhaps ten feet from the breech, reminiscent of home fireworks, catherine wheels, roman candles and the like – and, for scholars of Erasmus, the twisters that arrived unheralded, spiriting away worm masters to regions beyond our ken, leaving only mystery in their wake. Worm masters despised by *el capitán*, belatedly realising after a lifetime of struggle, he would never join that elect band, now bent on revenge and bringing the whole edifice of fiction down upon himself, firing the greatest store of gold ever assembled in Mexico, *oro* amassed since the conquest, the sweat of the sun and tears of more than a million slaves toiling their whole lives in absolute darkness. An appalling act of annihilation about to be witnessed by the federal troops assembled around the plaza, all the captives who had survived up to now, along with perhaps a thousand miners brought up from below, bringing down the sun on the world and ending a young master's dreams.

But not if a *generalísimo* had something to do with it. Panchito, at that moment hunched up in darkness, atop a great pile of gold, his chin resting on tremulous knees, hands clamped to his ears, eyes screwed shut, biting his lip as *el capitán*, a sardonic smile breaking out on his face, lit the long blue twist of paper and stepped back to admire his handiwork ...

There is no point even attempting to describe the awesome power of that detonation, the magnitude of the explosion, the force of the blast, sending the young master rocketing upwards in a shower of gold.

El capitán was no more. That evil genius intent on wiping the whole programme of fictions – crashing reality central – had been erased himself. Backfire from the breech, combined with the thunderous detonation reverberating the surrounding mountains brought half a little sister down on the town. The landslide, burying it deeper than Pompeii or even Herculaneum, preserving it for future archaeologists to mull over: the mystery of the giant bronze tubes with their odd serpentine stippling scattered around the plaza; the native miners and their oppressors, *federales* and *criollos*, all hostilities forgotten, cowering and defiant, huddled in groups, in attitudes of terror or acceptance. Perhaps the most poignant of the stifled lives, a *mestizo* trying to shelter his woman, in turn shielding their child, clutching a puppy to her chest, clenching in one fist a perfectly preserved revolutionary bill featuring the smiling face of a *generalísimo* on one side and a curious map on the other. All these wonders as nothing compared to the treasures of the cathedral, the great altar preserved completely intact, with its antependium of the flayed skin of the golden calf, with mummified Brethren of the Worm abasing themselves before it, their prayers unheard by the absconding young rascal who had dreamed up this world. But nowhere in the rubble was there found any trace of *el capitán*, annihilated by the wrath of a worm master, the back-blast from the breech, consuming him as if he had never been.

All this experienced by a retired captain, holed up in his book-lined study, hiding from Helga the harpy housekeeper in the presbytery of prescriptions, as a worrisome worm perturbation, a sudden shifting deep within his being, as if all the kabbalistic ciphers encrypting his mainframe programmes had in a flash been rewritten. Confused, he retired early to bed, not realising 'till morning he had suffered a stroke, when he became aware of a paralysis affecting his organs of speech. This perhaps the ultimate reason the young master was cast out to Elias Ashmole's Reformatory for Wayward Boys. Only once to see his father again, a shared loss made greater by their lack of communication, the hectoring pedant, transformed to a mumbler overnight. Hoarding words as misers hoard gold. Only by dint of enormous effort marshalling his forces, that one visit to the boarding school, very much the martinet, sitting upright with his black fedora shading his eyes in the back of his hired chauffeur driven car, ticking the lad off, telling him to mind his Ps and Qs, unable to conceal his irritation when the boy asked after his mother, the housekeeper having absconded with most of his stocks and shares – more than a lifetime's accumulations – since he had inherited the portfolio. The bitterness of the lengthy divorce case, settling like fallout, shrouding any happiness they'd shared in the past. Obliterating a far country as if it had never been, accessible only to a worm master, in his childish dreams of the orchards of the sun, playing with the three sisters he always wished he had ... Las Malinchés, sharing the same face, as only identical sisters can, waiting ... that next world, a worm away in Uncle Joe's *cantina* in the Town With No Name.

EPILOGUE

'Uncle?' That's what I said, the familial word, unbidden, spilling parched and gummy lips, as, prising sweat-sodden cheeks from the sticky tabletop, blurrily I made out a greying turkey buzzard, an ugly hooter, lumps and bumps breaking out all over, foreshortened and massive, pushing up to mine.

'At last you begin to guess at the truth of our relationship and my responsibilities towards you!' Joe beamed, clapping a spatula hand on my shoulder, setting another *mescal* on the table before me. '*Si*, I am your father's brother and, by the terms of the pact we made so long ago, his keeper also. Though I have to tell you I have been failing in that department recently.' Pausing, he laid a hand on heart. 'Not through any fault of my own,' he added gravely, 'But because Helga the hotelkeeper refuses to hand over his immortal remains.'

'Hold on a minute,' I gasped, gulping the contents of the tumbler, slopping *mescal* down my shirt front in my desperation to clear the fogs of a monumental hangover. 'When did you make this pact? And why?'

'It was after he rescued me from the only wadi in the whole of the Sinai Desert deep enough to drown a rat in. Even though your father was then serving as a captain in the British Eighth Army, at first took me for an Egyptian

176

spy, with the generosity that was the mark of his nature, gave me *el beso de la vida*.'

'You mean mouth to mouth?' I interjected, feeling the fogs clearing at last.

'*Es* the same,' Joe said, 'But I prefer *beso de la vida*, since it sounds so much better than *mano a mano*.' He lofted bushy eyebrows. 'How you say – resuscitation? It put me his debt and made us brothers, even though I hated his guts for the worm he had in there.'

'But what the hell were you doing? Drowning in the only wadi in the Sinai?'

'*Es* where blind chance dropped me.' Joe shrugged. 'I am surprised you have to ask, a worm master like you, knowing as you do of the holes between the worlds from all the adventures you have while snoring in my *cantina*.'

'Now I'm confused again,' I said, shaking my head, only partially clearing reforming fogs. 'You mean I've been here all the time?'

'All the time?' Joe tut-tutted just like a turkey. 'What sort of *loco* question is that for a worm master to ask?' I languidly raising a hand, he snapped fingers. 'Malinché,' he called without even bothering to turn round, 'Come and join us, and bring another *mescal*, *sans el gusano del diablo*, for my dear nephew here, and a *cervesa* for me.' Smiling steely, he leaned closer 'till our heads were almost touching. 'While we wait for the girls to do some work for a change, lees'en hard, and lees'en well,' he rasped. 'I have a message from your father.'

How many Mexicans does it take to pour a *mescal*? In the Town With No Name, at least three, on the evidence of my own eyes. Or perhaps I was seeing in triplicate, except there was only one bottle in view. The same impassive face, however, looming over – *las dos equis* and always looking for a 'Y', as Helga called them. The weird sisters. Las Malinchés, for the want of a better name.

'Allow me to introduce you,' Joe announced. 'Clotho, Atropos and Lachelis,' he chuckled wryly. 'Your sisters and everyone else's sisters.'

'Everyone's?' I reiterated. 'How is that possible?'

Joe shrugged. '*Cómo no*, dear nephew? When *es* the three fates stood before you.'

'Now I know I'm dreaming,' I said, giving each an enquiring look in turn, reciting names and assigning duties – just as my father declaimed Hesiod over my pram all those years before – 'Clotho, the spinner of the thread of life; Laesegis, blind chance, who determines the lot of every man; Atro ... po,' I stammered, noticing for the first time, the third sister was holding a pair of shears to her side, 'Who at the end cuts the thread ...'

Joe wasn't winding me up, or anything like that. Nor had my time arrived. The girls, or should I say Norns, were just being sociable, though at first it didn't seem that way. Their uniform expressions unchanging as they sat across the table, sipping iced Tia Maria in long glasses, staring into the middle distance dolefully. Sisters? Yes. Peas from the same pod. But confess I was distracted. That message Joe had passed on earlier preying on my mind.

'The crook at the end of the rainbow, *es* Meester Crook!'

'Come again Joe? Don't you mean crock?'

'No, crock *es* good, but Crook *es* better.'

'Are you trying to tell me my father's trusted advisor and most loyal friend has been up to no good?'

Snarling, Joe slammed a fist on the table. 'Now you begin to get the picture, dear nephew. All your problems trace back to that *cabrón*. The cause of your estrangement with your father, and your father's troubles with Helga.' He sighed mournfully. 'You know they murdered him, exactly as he predicted they would.'

'How?' I demanded.

'A leetle snake they slip into his bed.'

'Was it an asp by any chance?'

'So you do know something?' Joe's eyes narrowed.

'No.,' I shook my head, 'Just a remark my father once made about my mother. "Crocodile emotions with the bite of an asp".'

'Perhaps at last you understand, it was to protect you he sent you away to boarding school,' Joe said, placing a finger to his lips as *las Malinchés* loomed into view with our drinks.

Another *mescal* and another *mescal*, and I was beginning to get the picture. Time and their separate characters had wrought subtle changes on their physiognomy.

Clotho, despite her haughty mien – the mask she presented to the world – was the most remote of the sisters. Atropos, the coldest, possessing an icy radiance, chilling even at a distance. But in Laechelis I detected, or thought I did, a glimmer of interest behind her blind stare.

The all-knowing sisters. Blind to their brother before them, yet missing nothing. This the triumvirate of *brujas* who had overthrown my father. One little snip from Atropos' shears and his life was over. Even though I never knew, I knew. His passing preceded by portents diverse and multifarious, one of which was a dream, where he appeared at my door, and in abject tones, pleaded with me …

'To do what?'

'Die for me, young master, that I may live.'

'Fuck off!' I told him, appalled at what he was asking. 'After all you told me about the sisters, and you try to trick them in this way.'

It never did occur to me to complain that he hadn't been in touch for years.

But yet he pleaded, like Nebuchadnezzar, chewing the cud of his wasted days, on hands and knees, weeping saline tears, until I cast him out, into the teeth of that howling black gale. Damned but not quite out, my life hanging by a thread as, behind the scenes, *el capitán* attempted to renegotiate the deal.

Snip, snip. Even though I never knew, I knew. Those shears were closing and a male of the ancient Inkethaton line had to pay, Atropos would not be denied her quota.

Night-time-real-time, but dream-time yet, and I was walking across a city park, about to cross a path seemingly rolled over the sod, when suddenly I became aware of two tall and immensely thin men in black with beak noses approaching rapidly from either side – no sound accompanying their certain gait, their long steps equidistant and hypnotically matched as I approached the nexus, wanting to turn round and flee, but somehow unable. At the last moment, by enormous effort quickening my pace, passing through the closing gap, just before their trajectories crossed, feeling as I did so a thread shear away at my back, knowing then I had lost someone very dear. My father? How could that be? I hated the old bastard.

Another dream. A rolling verdant tapestry as wide as my life – at strategic intervals, playmates, playthings and a centrally placed clock, with the same scene racing across the dials, the sun and the waxing and waning moon alternating across the face. Along with a cavalcade of castles, hovels, milkmaids-a-milking and soldiers-a-drumming under passing clouds and pursuing stars. While above in a broader, bigger sky, my anguished father – *el capitán* no longer – looked up to the blue heavens with tears rolling his cheeks. Tears that were his last bequest and parting gift, as his imploring face faded from view, becoming pearls of the finest blue water, strung across the sky. And then I knew who had died, knowledge I retained on waking, even though I couldn't quite believe the colossus had fallen. The same day as I left New York for Mexico, on a mission to find the rest of my family, lost all these years.

Mexico, for Christ's sake, I'd never been there – except in my *loco* imagination perusing *The Picture Book of Mexican History*, yet at every turn of the trail, it all seemed so familiar – until I arrived in the town, encountered that murderous mother and swallowed the worm, ever after searching a maze of rooms and passages for a way out, desperate to escape my family – what was left of them – dead and alive, those that had been there at the beginning, there at the end, as the once-great tree withered, beset by *tzitzimimes*, harpies and conquistador dreams ... whole again, my little man *and* my nagual restored by the sacrifice of a double in a stone tree – a fair exchange in the circumstances. Writing this account for the want of something better to do.

Waiting for the day when the tunnel to the outside world would re-open and I could finally escape into the greater reality of Tláltipec.

One more thing about *el capitán*, my father in his altered worm state. What the fuck was he doing, you may ask, hanging out in *las tres hermanitas*? It's a good question. One day I suppose I'll find out, when at last I run out of thread and find myself under his command again – perish the thought – serving time in some theatre of combat or another. Who knows? Perhaps with the vanguard of sacrifices, doing battle against the astral armies of the stars and protecting the sun on its perilous journey through eternal night. Perhaps that's where I'll find him.

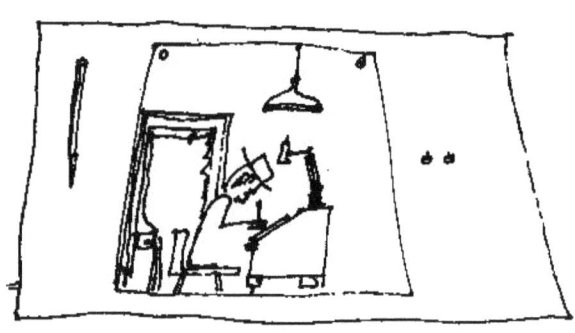

POSTSCRIPT

How much of the above is true? In the tradition of storytellers I'm tempted to say the lot, but I guess no one, no matter how credulous, could swallow that worm whole even if it happened to be the case. I am prepared to swear, however, on the bones of my beloved father, that the town, as represented, is accurate to the facts as I have been able to assemble. The precise name is another question, as is the treasure, or treasures – including a cache of gold coins stashed below a cathedral vault, all of which I wholeheartedly bequeath to that perspicacious reader who picks up on the clues and gets there first. As far as I am concerned you're welcome, just so long as you don't mention my name to that mother, still managing that renamed hotel.

Before I depart … There's one loose end that needs rolling. Remember the barrel-chested *borracho* with the most annoying nasal snicker sharing my seat, swapping sneers for cigarettes as the little bus ascended the cobbled road towards the tunnel, that first journey into town? I met him again, oddly enough, the same day I completed the first draft of the foregoing account, near to the summit of the highest of *los tres hermanitas*. Did I say near? I was yet a long way off, about to give up, with another few hours of hard slog before me, when he jumped out, from where I don't know – since there was a complete absence of cover in that vast plateau – and, sniggering madly in his idiosyncratic way, ran, shoved and dragged me to the top, where I promptly collapsed, the closest I've come to expiring, at least that's the way it felt. When I finally stood up, I could see neither hide nor hair of him for a hundred miles around. One thing I can report, however, is that, within a few feet of where he'd delivered me, was a solitary rose bush with the sweetest, most mellifluent perfume. Just one sniff enough to convince me that the divine is yet among us, and the arcadia of the Americas, known to the ancients as the garden of the golden apples of the sun, is much closer than I had thought.

More Novels by Will Lorimer,
published by Inkistan.com

TRANSEND
Before the Fall

As the Man said, 'It's our job to ensure the END has a time-table ... Events must be controlled. We can't just bow down to the inevitable!' The clock is ticking. Preparations are complete. Mountain refuges have been prepared for those with sufficient funds.

After the Fall ---

There's the CEO's billionaires, and Politicians living extended lives under the Mountain, whose status has been reduced to that of mere numbers.

There's the Punk saboteur, and her orange fireball sidekick, causing mayhem under the Mountain.

There's the fattest girl in the world who one day will be queen.

There's No. 1 and No. 3 in lockdown in a safe room, wondering what's going in the corridors beyond.

There's the phosphorescent dust thick in the air, which gets into everything, even miles underground.

There's the sclerotic eye which wanders the sky and beams down pestilence on the land below.

There's Bonaparte, only he's black – in charge of the Consensus, who thinks he rules the world.

There's the war between the Consensus, and the Trans-human rebels, as an even more precipitous Fall, looms.

ASIN: 1911289543 – (paperback) ASIN: B00WPV0E6M (KINDLE)

ON THE RUN IN DREAMTIME

The unlikeliest duo you'll encounter within the covers of a book or otherwise, Lobo and Frankie are the natural successors to Don Juan, and Carlos Castaneda, with a pinch of Laurel and Hardy for good measure. Lobo is a Swiss-Tibetan-playboy-mystic, who believes that Frank is the Chosen One. A pity then that the Chosen One should turn out to be a lazy, dirty mouthed Scotsman with as much mental clarity as a guinea pig, but Lobo is not deterred. Together they blaze an unstoppable trail across an unsuspecting Australia, in a pristine white falcon UTE – cruising the highways, sneaking the byways, and syphoning off gas pretty much everywhere. From the dives of Kings Cross Sydney, to the wild wastes of flying doctor country, they connive, conspire, and con their way in and out of trouble, in scenarios that Lobo creates to demonstrate the secret teachings of his master in a cave, back in Tibet. Along the road they encounter the gay queen of Melbourne, the gorgeous Renaldo Monte-Video, Nazis hiding out in a Queensland banana plantation when not on the Moon, fat necked outback cops, aborigine activists, lesbian truckers, and trans-hookers..

ASIN: 1838138250

The AWESOME
HeadfuX

Will Lorimer

Spanning worlds, realities, genres and possibilities, this counter factual novel begs the question - *what if* our reality is faux, all history bunkum, and the mind boggling conspiracy outlined within its pages, true? What if our culture is just an aggregation of stories recorded in the Book of Eternity? *What if* all the great scientists and savants are mere story tellers? *What if* this isn't a novel at all, but instead is the factual account of a nerve-racking tour of the multiverse, by way describing where we come from and are headed. -

KINDLE: ASIN: B00WPV0E6M - **Paperback.** – ASIN: 0956957765

the Last of the
Lutchens

THE ILLUSTRATED EDITION

Will Lorimer

(two editions, one illustrated)

Britain over the last hundred years, through the eyes of an Anglo-Scots family of dubious lineage, featuring the illusions and obsessions of three generations of the Lutchens, woven together in a genealogical tree rooted in a Scotland which we only thought we knew. Starting in the swinging sixties as the Beatles' first single tops the charts and the Cuban Crisis looms, the narrative tracks back through two world wars to uncover a skeleton in the family closet, before proceeding full circle, to when a national crisis threatens to break-up the disunited family. Will the Lutchens go their separate ways, or patch up their differences? Everything hangs in the balance for the family, and also the British nation state.

ASIN: B005F7TBEE (KINDLE) ASIN: B00MI574LS (KINDLE)

THE ESCAPE FROM MICTLÁN TRILOGY

- An Overview -
Alejandro Ehrenberg

It was a secret from his amnesic past that even his NY analyst couldn't decipher, which meant he had to go to Mexico in search of answers, specifically to a ghost town in the bandit-infested Sierra Madre, where his mother was waiting for him at the only hotel in town.

Deep in the Sierra Madre, behind a tunnel carved through the top of a mountain, one of the five that encircled the place like the fingers of a hand, is the strangest ghost town in Mexico. There is a hotel, run by a serial killer, and just across the street, a cantina, run by a drug cartel banker.

The town was founded in 1495, when a band of conquerors who, after the fall of Tenochtitlán, had been hunting the last Aztec eagle warriors in the mountains, found silver in the ashes of the previous night's fire. They were thirteen conquerors, whose descendants ruled the town for four hundred years, the richest in Mexico at the time, with a treasury, a mint, even an opera and of course a cathedral, until Pancho Villa and his North Division took the town in 1914 and shot the descendants of the conquerors, who took the location of the secret treasure to the grave.

After the Revolution, bands of adventurers from the four corners, lured by the legend of the Treasure of the Sierra Madre (some said there were thirteen treasures), dynamited most of the buildings of the medieval town — but of the treasure, or treasures, nothing was ever known. The Nahuas of the remote mountains think that it will never be known, as it is the property of the Lord of Death, king of Mictlán, and whoever discovers its location will be taken to one of the nine levels of the vast kingdom, which lies under the buried silver mines. in the mountains. This is the story of a search for answers, among which is what happened to a disgraced bishop, a damned enormously rich Kabbalist, who left for Mictlán with the secret of the treasures, where his prodigal bastard son has to go, if it is that he wants to decipher the enigmas of his amnesic past.

VOLUME 1

(Copiously illustrated by the Author, from his time researching the story in the peyote badlands of Northern Mexico.)

A prodigal bastard searching the remote Sierra Madre for the last whereabouts of his late father, tracks down the phillandering Bishops's former housekeeper, his mother who he suspects of being a serial killer, managing the only hotel in the *town with no name*, where nothing is as it seems, every day is the Day of the Dead, and the cathedral bells toll 13 at midnight. Even the Police chief has fled following the discovery of a mass grave under the bandstand in the main square, and the only safe place is the local cantina, where the barman is the narco-cartel banker.

KINDLE- ASIN: B08DXX9WF4 PAPERBACK - ASIN: 183813820X

VOLUME 2

WILL LORIMER

ESCAPE FROM MICTLÁN

A prodigal bastard's search for his father continues, from the Town with No Name, over the last unmapped mountain range in Mexico, to Narco HQ. Warmly welcomed by an old compadre, their reunion, however, is cruelly short when the evil Baron's black helicopters, swoop down on the hidden canyon and the narco-revolucinarios. Pursued into caverns, a *Generalissimo* disgraced, fleeing battle – cornered, he punges into a subterranean torrent and is swept away ... Eventually, to Mictlán, and his new employment under the terms of his contract with the presiding demon, as the Ferryman, on the Black River. Where it's true, dead men tell strange tales, and pay for the priviledge, in gold coin to a prodigal bastard, slowly punting the stiffs, shore to shore, to their last resting place in the wall of Nitches on the far side of Perdition - *once apon a time in Mictlán.*

KINDLE - ASIN: B08FG9JWN7

(The Spanish Language Edition of the Three
volumes, translated from the original English by
Alehandro Ehrenberg)

el
Espíritu que
jamás se entregó

Will Lorimer

ASIN: 1540139157

WOLFGANG: Volume 1

– BEWARE OF THE DOG –

Illustrated by the author

Enfant terrible, a freak of nature. His rise from obscurity to become Laird of **Castle Haggard,** following his marriage to Lady Brünhilda Constanze Haggard. **His travails** restoring the Castle. The **strange customs and traditions** of the Castle. Beset by demons disturbed by his renovations – a black dog, the Red Duchess, and vengeful ghosts. Betrayed in love - a laird cuckholded. The Laird's war against a drug baron and his henchmen. An encounter with Lucifer in the Black Pits. The riddle of the laird's map of shifting lines and the mystery of the famous hedge maze of **forking paths** of the Castle's famous vegetable garden. All this and more recounted in a series of tales, dictated to the laird's secretary, an untrustworthy Inuit, who has an even greater capacity for drugs than the laird himself, which is saying something.

Kindle - ASIN: B07XWBVLLZ - Paperback - ASIN: 169311028

BEWARE OF THE FOBY

- illustrated -

On the run from the authorities, Wolfgang's pursuit of the great novel continues, as he grapples with a world which is much changed since he last left the backwards Kingdom. America is no more, and new powers in the North compete for global domination. Meeting up with his untrustworthy amanuensis in London, he discovers she been playing away, and is back with Skull, his bitter enemy. Next, he learns he is under surveillance by Boreal Intelligence, and an international warrant has been issued for his arrest. Then, he unwittingly crosses an international crime family, and must make amends. Can he survive long enough to write the next volume, let alone complete the great work?

Kindle: ASIN:B087BT8HR7 Paperback: ASIN: 1911289551

DOG DAYS IN NEW YORK

A collection of short stories of life in Manhattan in the
early 1980's.
Illustrated by the Author.
Kindle – ASIN: B0883FTFYP –

NARRATED BY THE AUTHOR

MEET   THE

AUTHOR

Will Lorimer is a multimedia artist. He attended the
Scottish School of Hard Knocks and graduated with a
PHD in survival strategies.

To find out more about his Art
visit **Inkistan.com**

INKISTAN
.COM

www.ingramcontent.com/pod-product-compliance
Lightning Source LLC
Chambersburg PA
CBHW060809120626
46557CB00001B/147